WE'LL ALWAYS HAVE PARIS

BY

JESSICA HART

First published in Great Britain 2012
by Mills & Boon, an imprint of Harlequin (UK) Limited.
Large Print edition 2012
Harlequin (UK) Limited, Eton House,
18-24 Paradise Road, Richmond, Surrey TW9 1SR

© Jessica Hart 2012

ISBN: 978 0 263 22581 5

Harlequin (UK) policy is to use papers that are natural,
renewable and recyclable products and made from
wood grown in sustainable forests. The logging and
manufacturing process conform to the legal environmental
regulations of the country of origin.

Printed and bound in Great Britain
by CPI Antony Rowe, Chippenham, Wiltshire

For Isabel, dear friend and research advisor,
with love on her own Chapter Ten.

CHAPTER ONE

Media Buzz

We hear that MediaOchre Productions are celebrating a lucrative commission from Channel 16 to make a documentary on the romance industry. MediaOchre are keeping the details under wraps, but rumours are rife that an intriguing combination of presenters has been lined up. Stella Holt, still enjoying her meteoric rise from WAG to chat show host, says that she is 'thrilled' to have been invited to front the programme, but remains coy about the identity of her co-presenter.

One name being whispered is that of the economist, Simon Valentine, whose hard-hitting documentary on banking systems and their impact on the very poorest both here and in developing countries has led to a boom in micro-financing projects that is reputed to be revolutionising opportunities for millions around the world. Valentine, a reluctant celebrity, shot to fame with his crisp analysis of the global recession on the news, and has since become the unlikely pin-up of thinking women throughout the country. MediaOchre are refusing to confirm or deny the rumour. Roland Richards, its flamboyant executive producer, is uncharacteristically taciturn on the subject and is sticking to 'no comment' for now.

'NO,' SAID Simon Valentine. 'No, no, no, no, no. *No.*'

Clara's cheeks were aching with the effort of keeping a cheery smile in place. Simon couldn't see it on the phone, of course, but she had read somewhere that people responded more positively if you smiled when you were talking.

Not that it seemed to be having an effect on Simon Valentine.

'I know it's hard to make a decision without having all the facts,' she said, desperately channelling her inner Julie Andrews. *The Sound of Music* was Clara's favourite film of all time. Julie had coped with a Captain and seven children, so surely Clara shouldn't be daunted by one disobliging economist?

'I'd be happy to meet you and answer any questions you might have about the programme,' she offered brightly.

'I don't have any questions.' Clara could practically hear him grinding his teeth. 'I have no intention of appearing on your programme.'

Clara had a nasty feeling that her positive smile was beginning to look more like a manic grin. 'I understand you might want to take a little time to think about it.'

'Look, Ms…whatever you're called…'

'Sterne, but please call me Clara.'

Simon Valentine ignored the invitation. 'I don't know how to make myself clearer,' he said, his voice as tightly controlled as the image that stared out from Clara's computer screen.

She had been Googling him, hoping to find some chink in his implacable armour, some glimpse of humour or a shared interest that she could use to build a connection with him, but details of his private life were frustratingly sparse. He had a PhD in Development Economics—whatever *they* were—from Harvard, and was currently a senior financial analyst with Stanhope Harding, but what use was that to her? You couldn't get chatty about interest rates or the strength of the pound—or, at least, you couldn't if you knew as little about economics as Clara did. She had been hoping to discover that he was married, or played the drums in his spare time, or had a daughter who loved ballet or…something. Something she could *relate* to.

As it was, she had established his age to be thirty-six and the story of how he had quietly used his unexpected celebrity to revolutionize the funding of small projects around the world. So great had been the uproar in response to the programme he had written and presented that the big financial institutions had been forced to re-think their lending policies, or so Clara had understood it. She had read lots of stories from small collectives in sub-Saharan Africa, from farmers in South America and struggling businesses in South East Asia, as well as in the more deprived parts of the UK, all of whom had credited Simon Valentine with changing their lives.

It was all very impressive, but Simon himself remained an elusive figure. As far as Clara could see, he had been born a fully fledged, suit-wearing economist who had no interest in celebrity for its own sake.

There were no snaps of him staggering out of a club at four in the morning, no furtive shots of him shopping with a girlfriend. The ideal, of course, would have been some cheesy shots of Simon Valentine showing his 'lovely home' in the gossip mags, but Clara wasn't unreasonable. She had known that was a long shot, but she had thought she might at least find a picture of him at some reception, glass in hand.

But no. All she had was this corporate head and shoulders shot. He had the whole steely-jawed, gimlet-eyed thing going on, which Clara could sort of see the appeal of, although it didn't do much for her. His tie was straight and rigidly knotted, his jacket stiff, his shoulders squared. The guy had some serious control issues, in Clara's opinion.

Come to think of it, he had a definite Captain von Trapp quality to him, although he wasn't nearly as attractive as Christopher Plummer. *Obviously.* Still, Clara could imagine him summoning his children with a whistle.

Hmm. The thought gave her a definite frisson.

Perhaps a rousing rendition of *Edelweiss* would do the trick?

'Are you listening to me?' Simon Valentine demanded.

Hastily, Clara jerked her mind back from Salzburg. 'Of course.'

'Good, then I say this for one last time. I have no intention of appearing on your programme.' Simon spoke very distinctly and with exaggerated patience, as if addressing a naughty child. 'I don't need time to think about it now, just as I didn't need time when you emailed me the first time, or when you rang me for the fourth. My answer was no then, just as it's no now, and as it is always going to be. N. O. *No.* It's a very simple word. Do you understand what it means?'

Of course she understood. She might not be an academic like the rest of her family, but she had mastered the English language. It was Simon Valentine who didn't understand how important this was.

'If I could just expl—' she began desperately, but Simon, it appeared, had had enough explanations.

'Please do not try and call me again, or I will get very angry.'

And he cut the connection without waiting for her reply.

Clara slumped, making a face at the phone as she switched it off and tossed it onto the desk in defeat. *Now* what?

'Well? What did he say?'

She spun her chair round to see the director of *Romance: Fact or Fiction?* hovering in the doorway. 'I'm sorry, Ted,' she said. 'He's just not going to do it.'

'He's got to say yes!' Ted wrung his hands, the way he had been wringing them ever since Clara had first come up against a flat refusal from Simon Valentine. 'Roland's already promised Stella that Simon Valentine is on board!'

'Ted, I *know*. Why else do you think I've been harassing him?' But Clara was careful not to snap. Ted was one of her closest friends, and she knew how anxious he was about the new flat he and his partner had just bought.

More wringing of hands. 'What are we going to do?'

'I don't know.' With a sigh, Clara swung back to contemplate her computer screen. Simon Valentine gazed austerely back at her, the inflexible set of his lips taunting her with the impossibility of ever getting him to change his mind.

Puffing out a frustrated breath, Clara stuck her tongue out at him. Maturity was everything.

'Why can't Stella front the programme with someone else? Someone more approachable and more likely to take part? The Prime Minister, for instance, or—I know!—the Secretary General of the United Nations. Now there's someone who'd make a great presenter. I could give the UN a ring now...I'm sure it would be easier than getting Simon Valentine to agree.'

Her mouth turned down despondently. 'Honestly, Ted, I've tried and tried to talk to him, but he just isn't interested. You'd think he'd at least consider it after doing that programme on micro-financing, but he won't even let me explain.'

'Did you tell him Stella was super-keen to work with him?'

'I tried, but he doesn't know who she is.'

'You're kidding?' Ted gaped at her. 'I don't see how he could have missed her!'

'I don't get the impression Simon Valentine watches much daytime television,' said Clara, 'and I'm guessing the *Financial Times* doesn't devote much space to footballers' wives and girlfriends. This isn't a guy who's going to have a clue about celebrities.'

Ted grimaced. 'Better not tell Stella he's never heard of her or the fat really will be in the fire!'

'I can't think why she's so obsessed with Simon Valentine anyway,' grumbled Clara. 'He's so not her type. She should be going out with someone who's happy to be photographed all loved-up in *Hello!*, not a repressed economist. It's mad!'

Ted perched on the edge of her desk. 'Roland reckons she wants a relationship with Simon to give her gravitas,' he confided. 'Apparently she's desperate to shake off her WAG image and be taken seriously. Or maybe she just fancies him.'

'I just don't get it.' Clara studied Simon's photo critically. Even allowing for the vague Christopher Plummer resemblance, it was hard to see what all the fuss was about. Talk about buttoned-up!

'Did you hear that audience figures for the news have rocketed since he's been doing those analyses of the economic situation?' she said, mystified. 'Women all over the country have been switching on specially in the hope of seeing him, and now they're all tweeting each other about how sexy they think he is.' She shook her head at the photograph.

'They're calling him the Dow-Jones Darling now,' said Ted, and Clara snorted.

'More like the Nikkei Nightmare!'

'You ought to watch the news. You can't understand Simon Valentine's appeal until you've seen him in action.'

'I do watch the news,' Clara protested. She wasn't entirely superficial! She caught Ted's eye. 'Sometimes, anyway,' she amended.

'I made a point of watching the other night before I called him the first time so that I could tell him how brilliant he was—not that I ever got the chance to suck up,' she remembered glumly. 'I can see that he knows what he's talking about, but the whole he's-so-gorgeous thing has passed me by. He didn't smile once!'

'He's talking about the global recession,' Ted pointed out. 'Not exactly laugh-a-minute stuff. You can hardly expect him to be cracking jokes. What do you want him to say? Have you heard the one about the rising unemployment figures?'

'I'm just saying he doesn't look as if he'd be much fun.'

'Simon Valentine appeals to women's intellect,' said Ted authoritatively, and Clara rolled her eyes.

'Like you'd know!'

Ted ignored that. 'He's obviously fiercely intelligent, but he explains what's happening in the financial markets so clearly that you can actually understand it, and that makes you feel clever too. He only got invited to comment that first time because someone else wasn't available but he's a natural on camera.'

'I know. It's odd, isn't it? It's not as if he's incredibly good-looking or anything.'

'It's not about that,' said Ted with all the authority of a film director. 'It's about a complete lack of vanity. He clearly doesn't care what he looks like, and he's talking about a subject he's utterly comfortable with, so he's relaxed, and the camera loves that. I can see exactly why the BBC snapped up that documentary. There's a passion about the way he talks about economics…it *is* kind of sexy.'

'If you say so,' said Clara, unconvinced.

'It was Simon who sold the proposal when Roland pitched it to Channel 16. The suits loved the idea of putting him with Stella.'

Clara could just about get that. Stella Holt was a popular daytime television chat show host, famous for her giggle and revealing dresses. Who better to contrast with her than Simon Valentine, the coolly intelligent financial analyst who had somehow managed to make the global recession a sexy subject? The commissioning editors at Channel 16 had lapped it up, just as Roland Richards had said they would.

You didn't need to be Simon Valentine to know that the economic outlook was bleak for small television production companies like MediaOchre. They were incredibly lucky to have a programme commissioned at all, as Roland kept reminding them. If it wasn't for that, the whole company would be folding.

As it was, they had the money—an extraordinarily generous budget under the circumstances. They had Ted as an award-winning producer, and a camera and sound crew lined up. They had the locations chosen and deals set up with airlines and hotels. They had Stella Holt to add the celebrity glamour that would pull in the viewers.

All they needed was Simon Valentine.

As Roland also kept reminding Clara.

'You're the production assistant,' he told her. 'I don't care what you do, but get him on board or this whole thing is going to fall apart, and it won't just be you that's out of a job. We'll all be out on the streets!'

So no pressure then.

Remembering, Clara put her head in her hands. 'There must be some way of persuading Simon to take part. He won't talk on the phone or respond to emails… I need to talk to him face to face. But how?'

'Can't you get contrive to bump into him at a party?' Ted suggested.

Clara lifted her head to jab a finger at the screen. 'Does he look like a party animal to you? He doesn't do anything but work, as far as I can see. They even do those interviews in his office, so I can't even throw myself at him in the lift at the BBC.'

'He must go home some time. Hang around outside his office and then follow him.'

'Excellent idea. I could get myself arrested as a stalker. Although it might come to that. Anyway, he drives to work. It's very un-ecological of him,' said Clara disapprovingly.

They brooded on the problem for a while. Ted took the other chair and spun thoughtfully round and round, while Clara Googled in a desultory fashion.

'We could send a surprise cake to the office,' Ted suggested at last.

'And I could deliver it.' Clara paused with her fingers on the keyboard and considered the idea, her head on one side. 'I'd be lucky to get past reception, though.'

'I was thinking more of you jumping out of it,' said Ted, and she flattened her eyes at him.

'Oh, yes, he's bound to take me seriously if I jump out of a cake! Why don't I turn myself into a call girl and be done with it? And don't even *think* about mentioning that idea to Roland!' she warned, spotting the speculative gleam in Ted's eyes. 'He'll just make me do it.'

She turned back to the computer. 'Shame he doesn't appear to have any children. I could inveigle my way in as a governess and charm him into agreeing with my heart-warming song and dance routines.'

'You'd be better off pretending that you're setting up a weaving cooperative somewhere in the Third World,' said Ted, who was used to Clara drifting into *Sound of Music* fantasies. 'He's very hot on credit systems for small organisations that are struggling.'

'*We're* a small organisation that's struggling,'

Clara pointed out. 'Or we will be if he doesn't agree to take part!' She scrolled down the screen, looking for something, *anything*, that might help her. 'Pity he isn't hotter on self-promotion, but it's always the same story. It's about the projects, not about him—oh...'

Ted sat up straighter as she broke off. 'What?'

'It says here that Simon Valentine is giving a lecture at the International Institute for Trade and Developing Economies tomorrow night.' Clara's eyes skimmed over the announcement. 'There's bound to be drinks or something afterwards. If I can blag my way in, I might be able to corner him for a while. I'd have to miss my Zumba class, mind.'

'Better than losing your job.' Ted sprang up, newly invigorated. 'It's a brilliant idea, Clara. Wear your shortest skirt and show off your legs. Times are too desperate to be PC.'

Clara sniffed. 'I thought I'd dazzle him with my intellect,' she said, and Ted grinned as he patted her on the shoulder.

'I'd stick to my legs if I were you. I think they're more likely to impress Simon Valentine.'

Clara tugged surreptitiously at her skirt. She wished now that she had worn something a little more demure. Surrounded by a sea of suits in varying shades of black and grey, she felt like a streetlamp left on during the day in a fuchsia-pink mini-dress and purple suede killer heels. The other members of the audience had eyed her askance as she edged along the row and collapsed into a spare seat at the back of the room. On one side of her a brisk-looking woman in a daringly beige trouser suit bristled with disapproval. On the other, a corpulent executive leered at her legs until Simon Valentine began to speak.

There had been no problem about talking her way in without a ticket—Clara suspected the mini-dress had helped there, at least—but once inside it was clear that she was totally out of place. She fixed her attention on Simon, who was standing behind a lectern and explaining some complicated-looking PowerPoint presentation in a crisp, erudite way that appeared to have the audience absorbed.

It was all way over Clara's head. She recognised the odd word, but that was about it. Every now and then a ripple of laughter passed over the room, although Clara had no idea what had been so funny. She picked up the occasional word: percentages and forecasts, public sector debt and private equity. Something called quantitative easing.

Hilarious.

Abandoning her attempt to follow the lecture, Clara planned her strategy for afterwards instead. Somehow she would have to manoeuvre him into a quiet corner and dazzle him with her wit and charm before casually slipping the programme into the conversation.

Or she could go with Ted's suggestion and flash her legs at him.

Clara wasn't mad about that idea. On the other hand, it might be more effective than relying on wit and charm, and it would be worth it if she could stroll into the office the next day. *Oh, yeah*, she would say casually to Roland. *Simon's on board.*

Roland would be over the moon. He would offer her an assistant producer role straight away, and then, after a few thought-provoking documentaries, she could make the move into drama. Clara hugged the thought to herself. She would spend the rest of her career making spell-binding programmes and everyone would take her seriously at last.

A storm of applause woke Clara out of her dream.

OK, maybe an entire high-flying career was a lot to get out of one conversation, but she was an optimist. Climb every mountain, and all that. It could happen and, at the very least, convincing Simon Valentine to take part would save her job and mean that Ted could stay in his flat.

There was the usual scrum to get out of the room to the drinks reception afterwards. The International Institute for Trade and Developing Economies was as stuffy as its name suggested. It was an imposing enough building, if you liked that kind of thing, with elaborately carved plaster ceilings, portraits of stern Edwardian economists lining the walls, and a grand staircase that Clara longed to dance down. It was just begging for a sparkly dress and a Ginger Rogers impersonation.

The reception was held in the library and by the time Clara got in there the glittering chandeliers were ringing with the rising babble of conversation. Grabbing a glass of white wine, she skulked around the edges of the crowd, trying to look as if she understood what everyone was talking about. She recognized several famous journalists and politicians, and the air was thick with talk of monetary policy frameworks, asset bubbles and exchange rate policies.

Oh, dear, if only she was a bit more knowledgeable. She would never be able to dazzle Simon Valentine at this rate. Clara was careful to avoid eye contact with anyone in case they asked her what she thought about the credit crisis or interest rate cuts. She didn't want to be exposed as the imposter that she was.

The atmosphere was so intimidating that Clara was tempted to turn tail and go home before she was outed as utterly ignorant, but this might be her only chance to talk to Simon Valentine face to face. She *couldn't* go until she had at least tried. It would be too shaming to go into work the next day and admit that she'd lost her nerve.

Humming under her breath to bolster her confidence, Clara scanned the crowds for her quarry and spotted him at last, looking so austere in a grey suit that everyone else seemed positively jolly in comparison. Several women in monochrome suits of various shades were clustered around him, nodding fervently at everything he said. Those must be his groupies, thought Clara disparagingly, unable to see what it was about

Simon Valentine that made obviously intelligent women fawn over him.

Not that he seemed to be enjoying the experience, she had to concede. He had a definite air of being at bay, and she saw him steal surreptitious glances at his watch.

Seriously, the guy needed to relax a bit, Clara decided. He was holding a glass but not drinking from it and, as she watched, he put it back on a passing tray, offered a smile so brief it was barely more than a grimace to his disappointed fans and started to make his way out of the crush.

Terrified that he was leaving already, Clara drained her second glass for courage and headed after him. She couldn't let him get away without at least trying to buttonhole him.

Pushing her way through the crowds, she followed him out into the cavernous entrance hall in time to see him striding purposefully towards the cloakrooms. He was going to get his coat and leave, and her chance would be gone. She would have sat through a lecture on economics for nothing!

It was now or never.

Her heels clicked on the marble floor as she

hurried after him. 'Dr Valentine?' she called breathlessly.

Simon bit down on an expletive. His lecture had gone very well, but he would much prefer to have left immediately afterwards. Instead, he'd had to stand around and make small talk. He'd barely stepped into the library when a whole gaggle of women had descended on him. Ever since he had appeared on the news explaining the blindingly obvious about the financial situation, he had become a reluctant celebrity.

At first it had seemed an excellent idea. His firm was all for it, and Simon himself believed it was important for people to understand the economic realities of life. He had no problem with that, and the opportunity to bring new thinking about micro financing to global attention was too good to miss. He was delighted that the ensuing documentary had had such an impact, but had been totally unprepared for the effect of his television appearances on female viewers.

It was all very embarrassing, in fact, and the intent way some women had taken to hanging on his every word made him deeply uncomfortable. If they were that interested in economics, why didn't they go away and read his articles instead?

And now, just when he'd managed to escape for a few minutes' quiet, here was another one.

For a moment Simon considered pretending that he hadn't heard her, but some of his so-called fans could be annoyingly persistent, and he wouldn't put it past some of them to pursue him right into the Gents. So he paused, clenched his jaw, and fixed on his least welcoming expression.

But when he turned, the young woman coming after him didn't look at all like one of his normal fans, most of whom tended to hide their silliness at being fans in the first place beneath a veneer of seriousness. There was nothing serious about this girl.

His first impression was of vivid colour, his second of a spectacular pair of legs. In spite of himself, Simon blinked. He doubted very much that the Institute had ever seen a skirt that short before, or shoes that frivolous.

He allowed himself a moment to appreciate the legs before he made himself look away from them. Just because Astrid had left, he didn't have to start leering at the first pair of decent legs to come his way.

'Yes?' he said uninvitingly.

She offered him a friendly smile. 'I just wanted

to say that I enjoyed your talk very much,' she said, still breathless from the effort of hurrying after him in those absurd shoes. 'I thought you made some excellent points.'

Simon eyed her suspiciously. 'Oh? Which particular points?' he said. Maybe it was unfair to put her on the spot, but he didn't feel like being helpful.

'All of them,' she said firmly, only to falter as her gaze met his. She had an extraordinarily transparent expression, and Simon could see her realising that as an answer it was less than impressive and dredging up something she remembered from the lecture.

Which turned out to be not very much.

'What you said about qualitative easing was particularly interesting,' she offered with an ingenuous smile.

'Really? That's strange, as I was talking about *quant*itative easing.'

'That too,' she said.

He had to give her points for trying. Most of his 'fans' did their homework in an attempt to impress him when they met. This one clearly hadn't bothered.

'You're interested in the banks' asset policies?'

'Fascinated,' she said, clearly lying, but meeting his eyes with such limpid innocence that Simon felt an unfamiliar tugging sensation at the corner of his mouth. It took a moment before he recognized it as amusement, and he pressed his lips together before he actually smiled.

Now that he looked at her properly, he could see that she wasn't particularly pretty. Once you got past the animated expression, her features were really very ordinary, with ordinary brown hair falling in a very ordinary style to her shoulders. And yet she seemed to shimmer with a kind of suppressed energy, as if she were about to break into a run or fling her arms around, that made her not ordinary at all.

She made Simon feel vaguely unsettled, and that wasn't a feeling he liked.

'Were you even *at* my lecture?' he demanded.

'I sat through every riveting minute of it,' she assured him.

'And how much did you understand?'

He saw a brief struggle with her conscience cross her face before she opted, wisely, for honesty. 'Well, not everything…that is, not a lot… in fact, none of it, but I do admire you a lot, obviously.' She cleared her throat. 'The truth is, I don't know anything about economics. I'm here because I really need to talk to you.'

'I'm afraid I only talk about economics, so if you don't know anything about the subject it's likely to be a very short conversation,' said Simon curtly and made to turn away but she clutched at his arm.

'I won't keep you a minute, I *promise*,' she said and plunged into a prepared speech before he could shake his arm from her grasp. 'My name's Clara Sterne, and I—'

But she had already said enough. Simon's eyes narrowed. 'As in the Clara Sterne who has been ringing and emailing me and apparently doesn't understand the meaning of the word *no*?'

'Oh, you recognize my name? Good,' said Clara brightly.

Simon's mouth tightened. 'Spare your breath!' he said, flinging up a hand as she opened her mouth to go on. 'No, I will not participate in your ridiculous television programme. Once and for all… *No!*'

'But you haven't even given me a chance to explain about the programme,' she protested. 'It's not ridiculous at all. We want it to be a serious examination of the romance industry.'

'Clara, in case you haven't noticed, there's a global recession going on. I think there are more serious issues to examine than romance, even if such a thing existed.'

Clara pounced on that. 'So you don't think romance exists?'

She might as well have asked him whether he believed in the Jolly Green Giant. 'Of course I don't,' he said. 'It's clearly an artificial construct dreamed up by marketing teams.'

'Then that's all we want you to say on the programme! That's the whole point, in fact. It'll be a serious discussion, with you and your co-presenter putting different sides of the argument.'

'A serious discussion? I seem to recall you told me the other presenter was a footballer's wife who hosts a daytime chat show!'

'*Ex*-wife,' Clara corrected him. 'We think the contrast between the two of you will be very effective.'

She had an extraordinarily mobile face. Her eyes as she leant eagerly towards him were an undistinguished brown, but her expression was so bright that Simon was momentarily snared, like the proverbial rabbit in the headlights. Irritated by the image, he still had to make a physical effort to jerk himself free.

'I don't care how "effective" the contrast would be,' he said sharply. 'It's not going to happen.'

Clara regarded him in dismay. How could she persuade him if he wouldn't even listen to her? 'I'd have thought you would be pleased at the chance to convince people about your point of view,' she said. 'Your last documentary was really important, and we want this one to be the same.'

'My last documentary was about the alleviation of poverty! I hope you're not going to try and convince me the importance of that can be compared to *romance*?'

Uh-oh. Wrong track. Clara did some swift back-pedalling. 'No, of course not,' she said quickly. 'But we could offer the opportunity to do a follow-up programme on the projects you mentioned in your film,' she offered, seized by inspiration, and mentally crossing her fingers that Roland would agree. 'It would be great publicity for you.'

But that was the wrong thing to say too. 'I'm not interested in publicity,' said Simon quellingly. 'I'm interested in making systems work so that the people who need help get it. It's nothing—'

He broke off, obviously catching sight of someone over Clara's shoulder, and stiffened.

Curious, she turned to see a couple coming towards them. The woman was coolly elegant, her companion dark and Mediterranean-looking and seriously hot.

There was an awkward pause, then the woman said, 'Hello, Simon.'

'Astrid.' Simon inclined his head in curt acknowledgement, his voice clipped.

Clara looked from one to the other with interest. There was something going on here. Astrid was rather lovely, Clara thought enviously, with perfect skin, perfect bone structure and a perfect shining curtain of silvery-blonde hair.

And no prizes for guessing Simon thought so too. He was looking wooden but Clara prided herself on reading body language and, unless she was much mistaken, Astrid was an ex of some kind.

'You haven't met Paolo before.' Astrid sounded composed enough, but there was a telltale flush along her cheekbones as she introduced the two men, who eyed each other with undisguised hostility. 'Paolo Sparchetti, Simon Valentine.'

'Ciao,' drawled Paolo, and put a possessive arm around Astrid's waist.

Lucky Astrid, was all Clara could think. Paolo was sulkily handsome, with a wide sensuous mouth and just the right degree of stubble to make him look sexily dishevelled. Now if *he* was commenting on the stock markets, she might take an interest in the economy. It was bizarre to think that Simon was the one with all the fans.

Simon was definitely jealous. He barely managed a jerk of his head to acknowledge the introduction.

Ver-rr-ry interesting, thought Clara.

It was hard to imagine two men more different. Simon was all buttoned up and conventional, while Paolo was smouldering passion in an open-necked shirt and a designer jacket, with a man purse slung over his shoulder. Clara was prepared to bet her life on the fact that Simon would die rather than carry a handbag.

There was another taut silence.

Clara looked from one to the other, intrigued by the fact that Astrid seemed torn. Her body seemed to be attuned to Paolo's—and, frankly, Clara didn't blame it—but her mind was apparently focused on Simon's reaction.

Hmm. Clara scented an opportunity. Somehow she needed to get Simon and Astrid back together, which would make Simon so grateful that he would offer her, Clara, anything she wanted in return for restoring his lost love to him. At which point she would mention MediaOchre's pressing need for him to appear in the programme.

Of course I'll do it, he would say. *Anything for you, Clara.*

Well, it was worth a shot.

CHAPTER TWO

CLARA considered her options. She could try and draw Paolo's attention away from Astrid, but that was frankly unlikely. Clara could scrub up well enough when she tried, but she had none of Astrid's cool beauty.

The alternative was to make Astrid jealous of Simon.

It shouldn't be too hard, Clara decided. A look, a hint, a suggestion that Simon had found someone else ought to be enough.

All she had to do was pretend to be in love with Simon.

And how hard could that be?

Years earlier, when she had still been dreaming of making it to Broadway, Clara had done a drama course. Her acting career had been humiliatingly short, but she could still pull out the stops when she tried.

Putting on a bright smile, she stepped just a

little closer to Simon and stuck out her hand to Astrid. 'Hello, I'm Clara.'

It was pretty clear that Astrid hadn't registered Clara's presence up to that point. Clara wasn't offended. If she had Paolo on her arm, she wouldn't notice anyone else either, and it wasn't as if Clara was a likely rival for his interest, more was the pity.

Still, Astrid's perfect brows drew together as she took in Clara's appearance, and when her perfect green eyes reached the hem of Clara's mini-dress, the perfect mouth definitely tightened.

'Hello,' she said with marked coolness.

Clara pretended not to notice. 'Simon was *brilliant*, wasn't he?' She threw Simon an adoring look.

The feedback at the end of her drama course had been succinct: stick to dancing. If only her tutors could see her now! They might change their minds about her acting abilities. She deserved a gleaming statuette at least for convincing Astrid that she was starstruck by Simon Valentine, Clara decided.

'I've just felt so *inspired* about the economy since meeting Simon,' she cooed. 'I've learnt so much, haven't you?'

Simon unfolded his lips. 'Astrid is a hedge fund manager.'

Clara didn't have a clue what a hedge fund manager was, but she gathered from Simon's tone and Astrid's expression that there was little the other woman had to learn about economics.

'How exciting,' she said, bestowing a kind smile on Astrid. 'Did you enjoy Simon's lecture anyway?'

'Of course,' said Astrid. She glanced from Clara to Simon. 'I've heard him talk before, obviously.'

Obviously.

'It's still a thrill for me every time.' Clara thought that was a clever touch, hinting that she had sat through hours of economic lectures just for the pleasure of listening to Simon's voice. Talk about devoted!

Astrid hesitated. 'I just thought it would be a good idea for you and Paolo to meet, Simon,' she said, effectively cutting Clara out of the conversation.

It was Clara's cue to make an excuse and leave, but instead she put a hand on Simon's arm and beamed at the other two, not budging. 'It's lovely to meet *you*,' she assured them, very aware of Simon, who had gone rigid at her touch.

Baulked of the tête-à-tête she so plainly desired, Astrid had to concede defeat. 'Well, I'll see you in the office tomorrow,' she said to Simon, pointedly ignoring Clara. 'Paolo, we'd better go.'

'Whenever you want, *cara*.' The smirk Paolo sent Simon was a classic, and Simon glowered after the Italian as he sauntered off with Astrid.

'Did you see that?' he demanded. 'She's actually with a man who carries a handbag!'

She had got that right, anyway. 'I think you'll find they're called carry-alls,' said Clara.

'It looked like a handbag to me,' snarled Simon. Then he remembered who he was talking to, and rounded on her.

'And what did you think you were doing barging in on a private conversation, anyway?'

The brown eyes looked guilelessly back at him. 'I thought you'd be glad of my help.'

'Help?' He glowered at her. 'What for?'

'You want Astrid back, don't you?'

'What?' Simon was completely thrown. 'How did you know that?' he asked involuntarily and then glowered some more, furious with himself for such a revealing remark.

'Well, you *could* have hung a sign saying "jealous loser" round your neck,' said Clara, evidently quite undaunted by his thunderous expression, 'but otherwise it's hard to see how you could have made it more obvious!'

Feeling his mouth fall open in a gape, Simon snapped it shut. Who *was* this girl? She had some nerve, he had to give her that! Nobody else he knew—apart from his mother, perhaps—would think of talking to him that way.

'Astrid didn't like me being with you, you know,' she went on knowledgeably.

'You're not with me!'

'But she doesn't know that, does she?'

Simon was beginning to wonder if he was having a particularly vivid and unsettling dream. His life was black and white and firmly under control. He didn't talk about relationships. He didn't let himself get trapped into bizarre conversations with young women who wore vibrant colours and inappropriately short skirts and who appeared to have no compunction about barging in on other people's conversations or offering unsolicited advice.

'Any fool can see why Astrid is with Paolo— I mean, he's seriously hot—but she's clearly still got a thing about you.' Clara couldn't quite manage to keep the bafflement from her voice,

Simon noted. 'Instead of you glaring at Paolo, you need to make *her* jealous.'

'Jealous?' echoed Simon, even as he wondered why he was even having this conversation.

Clara nodded encouragingly. 'Make her wonder what she's missing,' she said.

'And this is any of your business because…?'

'Like I say, I can help you. I don't mind hanging around and simpering at you whenever you're likely to meet Astrid. She won't like the idea that you're with me at all, and if you can't make the most of the situation when she tells you how jealous she is, I wash my hands of you.'

Unbelievable. What kind of world was Clara Sterne living in? Simon regarded her with his most sardonic expression.

'And in return for this sacrifice on your part? Or can I guess?'

'Well, you're not stupid,' said Clara, 'so yes, you probably can. All you'd have to do in return is present a one-hour film.' She looked at him hopefully. 'Well? Do we have a deal?'

She didn't seriously expect him to agree to that nonsense, did she? Ruin his reputation as a serious economist by taking part in some sentimental twaddle?

'Not exactly,' said Simon, 'but I do have a deal to offer *you.*'

He crooked a finger in conspiratorial fashion and her face lit up. 'Really?' she said, leaning closer. Simon got a whiff of a fresh citrusy scent.

'Really,' he said.

'What's the deal?'

'It's a very simple one. *You* go away and leave me alone, and *I* won't call Security to throw you out. How's that for an offer?'

Clara recoiled in disappointment. 'Oh, but *please...*'

Unmoved by the pleading brown eyes, Simon looked at his watch. 'I'll count to ten, then I'm calling Security.'

'All right, I'm going!' she said hastily. Digging in her purse, she produced a business card and pushed it into his hand. 'But here are my contact details, just in case you change your mind.'

Shaking his head with a mixture of exasperation and reluctant admiration at her persistence, Simon permitted himself a last look at her legs as she left, clearly disappointed but still with plenty of verve to the swing of her hips. As the click of those precipitous heels faded and she disappeared around the corner, he found that he was turning her card round and round between his fingers, and he stopped himself irritably.

Clara Sterne, Production Assistant, Media-Ochre Productions, the card read. Who in God's name would want to have anything to do with a company that called itself MediaOchre? The name was either prescient or indicated an ominous taste for puns. Simon had no intention of getting involved either way.

Unable to spot a bin, he shoved the card in his jacket pocket. He would dispose of it later, as he certainly wouldn't be needing it. That was the last he would see of Clara Sterne.

Simon drummed his fingers on his desk. When they were going out, it had been very convenient that Astrid worked in the same office, but now it felt…well, awkward.

Simon didn't *like* feeling awkward. He had always liked the fact that it had been so *comfortable* being with Astrid. She didn't make scenes or get all emotional, and she never got personal in the office.

So why she wanted to spoil it all by throwing everything up for a pretty Italian, Simon couldn't begin to fathom. He thought she had been happy with him. She had *said* she had been happy. And then one day it had been all about being swept off her feet and wanting 'passion' and 'romance'.

Madness.

Astrid had put her head round his door earlier and asked if she could have a word. He'd been glad to see her. If they could have sat down together and chatted about financial sustainability for NGOs or risk analysis, he was sure she would have remembered how much better off she was with him. It wasn't as if she could have a meaningful conversation with a man who carried a handbag, after all. Surely she would get bored with Paolo soon?

Not that he was jealous, whatever Clara Sterne had had to say about it. That was nonsense. He didn't get jealous. That wasn't how he and Astrid had operated, and he wasn't about to start now.

Simon had every faith that Astrid would come to her senses but, apparently, it wasn't yet. She had no time for economic policy nowadays, and was determined to talk about bloody Paolo instead. How he made her feel. How guilty she then felt about Simon. Feelings, feelings, feelings… Simon couldn't understand it. It was so unlike her.

Now Astrid was pacing. That was another thing she had never used to do.

'Who was that you were with last night?' she asked abruptly.

'Last night?'

'That girl. Clara. I got the impression she was with you.'

Simon opened his mouth to deny any acquaintance with Clara Sterne, but the words died on his tongue as her words came back to him.

She's clearly still got a thing about you. Instead of glaring at Paolo, you need to make her jealous.

Was it possible that Clara was right?

Simon was unsettled by how clearly he could remember her. Clara wasn't a beautiful woman like Astrid, of course, but there had been a sort of quirky appeal to her undistinguished features, he had to admit. Something to do with the warm brown eyes, perhaps, or that mouth that seemed permanently tilted at the corners.

Or maybe those spectacular legs.

Simon was prepared to admit to a sneaking admiration for her daring, too, if he were honest, although he had no intention of changing his mind.

In his jacket pocket he'd found her card, which

he'd forgotten to put in the bin. Now he turned it on the desk, frowning slightly.

'How long have you known her?'

To his relief, Astrid stopped pacing and sat down on the other side of his desk. A tiny crease had appeared between her immaculately groomed brows.

'Not long.' Simon shifted, uncomfortably aware that he wasn't being entirely truthful.

'It's just that I worry about you,' Astrid said unexpectedly. 'I know we're not together any more, but that doesn't mean I don't care about you, and I'd hate it if you were to do anything foolish.'

Simon paused in the middle of turning the card on its side. 'Foolish?' Pretty rich coming from someone who had thrown over a perfectly satisfactory relationship for a handbag-carrying Italian!

'Clara's very...' Astrid paused delicately '...*colourful*, but she's hardly your type, Simon. And that dress! Totally inappropriate, I thought.'

It had been, but Simon couldn't help remembering how good Clara's legs had looked in it.

'I know you're too intelligent to be taken in by a girl in a miniskirt,' Astrid went on, 'but I hope you'll be careful.'

'I'm always careful,' said Simon.

It was true. He liked his life firmly under control. Risk analysis was his speciality. He didn't do reckless or spontaneous. And he certainly didn't do foolish. He'd seen just how disastrous recklessness and foolishness could be, and neither were mistakes he would be making.

'I know.' Astrid's expression softened. 'Look, it's hard to talk about these things in the office. Why don't we meet for a drink later?' Then, just when he was congratulating himself on being right about her returning to her senses, she spoiled things by adding, 'I'd really like you to get to know Paolo.'

So much for a quiet drink sorting things out. Simon wanted to be with Astrid, but he had no desire to get to know any more about Paolo. As far as he was concerned, he already knew more than enough.

'I'm sorry, Astrid,' he said, 'but my mother is coming to town this evening, and I promised to take her out to dinner. I'm expecting her any minute, in fact. Another time, perhaps.'

Preferably when Paolo was unavailable.

As if on cue, his PA buzzed him from her office.

Not sorry for the distraction, Simon flipped the switch. 'Yes, Molly?'

'I've just had a call from Reception,' said Molly. 'Your mother's there. She's fine, but there's been some kind of incident. Could you go down?'

When the lift doors opened, Simon spotted his mother straight away. She was at the centre of a cluster of people on the far side of the atrium, but when she saw him she hurried over to meet him. 'Thank goodness you're here!'

Simon's brows snapped together at the sight of her flustered appearance. Frances Valentine was still an attractive woman, but now her highlighted blonde hair was dishevelled, and there were spots of colour in her cheeks. 'What on earth has happened?'

'I've been mugged!' she announced with her usual flair for the dramatic.

'Are you all right?' he asked in quick concern.

'I'm fine. It's Clara I'm worried about.'

'Clara?'

'She saw what happened, and tackled the mugger,' Frances said admiringly, tugging him over to a bedraggled figure sitting on one of the low leather sofas, nursing one arm. 'Wasn't it brave of her?'

With a sinking sense of inevitability, Simon recognized the long legs first. His gaze travelled up over the torn tights, mud-splattered skirt and top to a face that was already unsettlingly familiar. Above the colourfully striped scarf that was wound several times around her neck, Clara Sterne's face was paler than the night before but, even shaken, she managed to look more vivid than the other women clucking over her and, as her brown eyes widened at the sight of him, he felt an odd little zing pass through him.

'*You're* Frances's son?' she exclaimed.

'You know each other?' his mother said in delight.

'No,' said Simon.

Just as Clara said, 'Yes.'

How did a woman as warm and friendly as Frances have a son as stiff as Simon Valentine? Clara wondered. She hadn't been expecting to see him just then, and surprise had sent her heart jumping into her throat at the sight of him.

At least she hoped it was surprise.

He looked as disapproving as ever, as if she had thrown herself into that puddle and torn her tights and hurt her wrist just to annoy him. She had wanted to see him, of course, but not like this.

'What happened?' he asked his mother.

Frances launched into her story. 'I was just crossing the road when I felt this thump on my shoulder and this awful oik grabbed my bag.' She shuddered. 'I got such a fright! It's my favourite bag too. Do you remember I bought it in Venice last year?'

Judging by Simon's expression, he knew nothing about his mother's handbags and cared less. Clara saw him keeping a visible rein on his impatience.

'How did Clara get involved?'

'She saw what was happening.' Frances sat down next to Clara and patted her knee. 'Lots of other people must have seen too, but no one else moved. Clara took off after him straight away, and she got hold of my bag, but they had a bit of a tussle and he pushed her to the ground before he ran off.'

Drawing breath, she looked up at her son. 'I'm very much afraid she may have broken her wrist, but she says there's no need to call an ambulance. You try and talk some sense into her, Simon.'

'There's no need, really.' Clara managed to get a word in at last. 'I'm perfectly all right. I can walk.'

'You're not all right! Look at you. You've ruined your tights, and I can tell your wrist is hurting.'

It was. When the mugger had shoved her, Clara had lost her balance and her wrist had taken the whole weight of her body as she fell. But her legs were all right, thank goodness, and she hardly counted as an emergency.

'I'll get a taxi,' she compromised.

'You'll do no such thing!' said Frances roundly. 'Simon has a car. You'll take her to hospital, won't you, darling?'

Clara had never seen anyone look less like a darling than Simon Valentine right then. It was almost worth a sore wrist and scraped knees to see the expression on his face, where impatience, frustration and reluctance warred with the mixture of exasperation and affection he obviously felt for his mother.

'Of course,' he said after a moment.

'Really, it's not necessary…'

'Nonsense!' said Frances. 'You're a heroine, and so I shall tell the police.'

'All right.' Rather to Clara's relief, Simon interrupted his mother's account of her heroics and took charge. Her wrist was getting more painful by the minute, and she was glad to be able to sit numbly while he despatched the cluster of receptionists who had been clucking ineffectually and arranged for his mother to be taken to his home in a taxi.

Only then did he turn his attention to Clara.

'There's no need to look at me like that,' she said as she got stiffly to her feet.

'Like what?'

'Like you think I arranged the mugging on purpose.'

'It crossed my mind.' Simon pushed the button for the lift to take them down to the basement car park. 'If you were desperate enough to sit through a lecture on monetary policy, who knows what you'd be prepared to do.'

'I was desperate to talk to you, but not quite desperate enough to tackle a mugger,' said Clara. She didn't add that Roland would certainly have pushed her into it if he thought it would get results.

As it appeared to have done. She mustn't waste this opportunity, she told herself, but her knees were stinging where she had grazed them and the pain in her wrist made it hard to concentrate.

Simon looked at her sideways as the lift doors slid open and they stepped inside.

'And yet you did it anyway. It was a dangerous thing to do. What if the mugger had been armed?'

'I didn't think,' Clara confessed, cradling her forearm. 'I saw your mum stagger, and then this young guy snatched her bag. It just made me mad. She looked so shocked that I ran after him and grabbed the bag back.'

She was very aware of him in the close confines of the lift. He seemed bigger than he had the night before. Stronger and more solid. More male. More overwhelming, and she found herself babbling.

'It would have been fine if he'd just let me take the bag back,' she rattled on. 'I suppose that was too much to hope after he'd gone to all the trouble of stealing it. Anyway, he turned round and shoved me, and the next thing I was crashing into a puddle.'

She grimaced down at herself. Her favourite skirt was ruined. 'I kept hold of the bag, though, and everyone was looking by then, so I think he just cut his losses and ran off. Your mother had caught up with us by then, so I was able to give her the bag back. She insisted that we come in here, but I honestly didn't know that you were her son!'

'I believe you,' said Simon with a dry glance. The lift doors opened, and they stepped out into the garage. 'But I hope you're not going to ask me to believe that it was coincidence that you were outside the building?' he asked, leading the way to a sleek silver car.

'No.' Clara didn't see any point in denying it. 'I was hoping to catch you when you left work. I thought you might be in a better mood today.'

Simon jabbed the key in the direction of the car to unlock it. 'I was in a perfectly good mood yesterday!' he said as the lights flashed obediently. 'Just as I'm in a perfectly good mood today,' he added through clenched teeth, opening the passenger door for her with pointed courtesy.

'Gosh, I hope I never meet you in a bad mood,' said Clara.

There was a dangerous pause, and then Simon shut the door on her with a careful lack of emphasis.

'I'm grateful to you for going to my mother's rescue,' he said stiffly when he got behind the wheel and started the engine, 'but if you're thinking of using this situation to press your case about this wretched programme of yours, please don't bother. I'm not changing my mind.'

Clara heaved a martyred sigh. 'All right. My wrist is too sore to grovel right now, anyway.' She slid him a glance under her lashes. 'I guess I'll just have to resign myself to pain and the prospect of losing my job.'

'You know, there is such a thing as employment law,' said Simon, unimpressed. 'They can't sack you because you had an accident and hurt your wrist.'

'No, but they can for failing to do your job, which in my case was to get you to agree to present the programme.'

'Emotional blackmail.' Simon put the car into gear and drove up the ramp and out into the dark January evening. 'The perfect end to a perfect day.'

'You're right.' Emotional blackmail was all she had left. 'It's not your problem if my career is over, or if I can't pay my rent and have to go back to live with my parents and admit I'm a total failure.'

Simon spared her a brief glance. 'Save it,' he advised. 'If you've done your research, you'll know that I'm completely heartless.'

'I have, and you're not,' said Clara. 'I know how many times you've volunteered for emergency relief projects after disasters. A heartless person doesn't do that.'

'Don't make me into a hero,' he said curtly. 'I'm not getting my hands dirty. I just make sure the money gets to those who need it.'

Quite a big 'just', Clara would have thought. Simon might not be pulling people out of the rubble or a doctor saving lives, but he regularly left his comfortable life in London to spend several weeks in extremely difficult conditions. Nothing happened without money, and relief efforts depended on financial managers like him to channel the funds where they were most needed and stop them being siphoned off by fraud and corruption.

Simon was clearly anxious to change the subject. 'Besides,' he said, cutting across her thoughts, 'it's totally unreasonable for anyone's job to depend on one person.'

'Tell that to my boss,' said Clara glumly.

'They must be able to find someone else. It's not even as if I'm a professional broadcaster.'

'It has to be you.' Faced with his intransigence, she had nothing to lose, Clara decided. She might as well be straight. 'The budget is based on your participation, and Stella Holt won't take part unless you do. The whole thing falls apart without you,' she told him. 'And so does MediaOchre. There are only three of us as it is. That's why I've been so persistent.'

'Basing the entire future of a company on one individual is an extremely risky economic strategy,' said Simon severely.

'I suppose so, but you have to take a risk every now and then, don't you?'

She knew immediately she had said the wrong thing. Simon's expression didn't change, but she felt him withdraw, like a snail shrinking back into its shell, and his voice was distant. 'Not in my experience,' he said.

There was a pause. 'Well, you can't say I haven't tried,' she said after a moment.

'No,' said Simon, 'I can't say that.'

A dreary drizzle misted the windscreen, and the streetlamps cast a fuzzy orange glow over the commuters hurrying for the tube, collars turned up against the cold and the damp.

How was she going to break it to Ted and

Roland? Clara's heart sank. She had failed them both. Now she could wave goodbye to her shiny new career and her hopes of becoming a producer. Just when she had filled the aching gap in her life left by Matt and found something she really wanted to do too.

Where was Julie Andrews when she needed her? As so often, Clara opted for frivolity when things looked like getting desperate. It was better than the alternative, which was crying hopelessly and which never really helped anyway. That was a lesson she had learnt the hard way in the weeks and months after Matt had left.

Well, she would just have to cheer herself up. Clara hummed a few bars of *My Favourite Things* under her breath while Simon negotiated an awkward junction.

'What are you doing?'

'Singing to myself.'

'What on earth for?'

'To make myself feel better.' It seemed obvious to Clara.

'I thought that's why I was taking you to hospital.'

'Music is the best medicine,' she said. 'Musicals taught me that.'

She might as well have claimed to have learned it from aliens. 'Musicals?' asked Simon as if he had never heard the word.

'Shows where the actors sing and dance around,' said Clara helpfully. 'And some of the greatest movies ever made. Take *The Sound of Music.* You must have seen that?'

'I've heard of it.' He eased into a gap between a bus and a taxi.

'I'll bet you know most of the songs.' She hummed the tune again. 'Is it ringing any bells?'

Simon glanced at her, shook his head slightly, and turned his attention back to the traffic. 'I have no idea what you're talking about, Clara.'

She gaped at him, astounded by his ignorance. This was probably how he felt about anyone who didn't know all about quantitative easing and interest rate policies.

'It's a classic song,' she told him. 'And, what's more, it really does work. When things go wrong—like you refusing to take part in the programme and ruining my career, for instance—all I have to do is sing a bit and I instantly feel better.'

It had worked when she missed Matt. Most of the time.

'Who needs a doctor when you've got *The*

Sound of Music?' she said cheerfully, and Simon shook his head in disbelief.

'I think I'd still take my chances at the hospital if I were you.'

At least three of the nurses in the A and E department recognized Simon, and there was a rather unseemly tussle as to who would help him. Initially triumphant at securing the task of dealing with Clara, the staff nurse was positively sulky when she realised that Simon planned to wait outside, and that the other two were left to fuss around him.

Not that Simon even seemed to realise that he was getting special treatment. 'I'll be here when you're ready,' he said to Clara. Taking a seat on one of the hard plastic chairs, he unfolded the *Financial Times* and proceeded to ignore everyone else.

By the time she emerged with a plaster cast up to her elbow and her arm in a sling, Clara was tired and sore and feeling faintly sick. She wanted Matt. Usually she was very good at persuading herself that she was fine, but at times like this, when her defences were down and she just needed him to put his arms round her and tell her that everything would be all right, his absence sharp-ened from a dull ache to a spearing pain.

Matt wasn't there for her any more. There was no one there for her.

Except Simon Valentine, who was sitting ex-actly where she had left him, and the rush of relief she felt at the sight of him made her screw up her face in case she burst into tears or did something equally humiliating.

'The sister said your wrist is broken,' he said, folding his newspaper and getting to his feet as she appeared. 'I'm sorry, it must be very painful.'

Clara put on a bright smile. She wasn't going to be a cry-baby in front of Simon Valentine.

'It's not too bad.' She moved her arm in its sling gingerly. 'I have to come back to the fracture clinic in a week, and they'll put a lightweight cast on it then.'

'My mother rang while you were being X-rayed,' he told her. 'It seems she picked up your bag when you dropped it to go after that mugger.'

Clara clapped her good hand to her head. 'Thank goodness for that! I forgot all about it in all the kerfuffle.'

'We'll go and pick it up, and then I'll take you home.'

'Honestly, I'm fine,' she said quickly. 'I can get a cab.'

'You might as well resign yourself,' he said. 'My life wouldn't be worth living if my mother got wind of the fact that I let you go home in a taxi!'

His suit was still immaculate, and she was horribly aware all at once of her scuffed knees and mud-splattered clothes where she had fallen. His hand was strong and steadying through her jacket as he took her good arm and steered her out through the doors to the car park, and she was guiltily grateful to his mother for insisting that he go with her to the hospital.

Being driven was a luxury too, she thought, sinking into the comfortable leather seat. It certainly beat the tube, or squeezing onto a bus with everyone else, coats steaming and breath misting the windows.

'You don't strike me as a man who's scared of his mother,' she said, turning slightly to look at him as he got in beside her.

'She has her own ways of getting what she wants,' said Simon in a dry voice. 'I've learnt it's easier just to do what she says.'

Throwing his arm over the back of her seat,

he reversed out of the narrow parking slot. Clara sat very still, afraid to move her head in case she brushed against him. All at once it felt as if there wasn't quite enough oxygen in the car.

'I thought she was charming,' she said breathlessly.

'Oh, yes, she's charming,' he said with a sigh and, to Clara's relief, he brought his arm back to put the car into forward gear once more. 'Great fun, wonderful company and completely irresponsible, but she gets away with it. She can be utterly infuriating, but if you try and reason with her, she just smiles and pats your cheek and, before you know where you are, you're doing exactly what she wants.'

Now why hadn't she thought of patting his cheek? Clara wondered. Somehow she felt it wouldn't have worked for her.

She liked the sound of Frances, though. She seemed a most unlikely mother for Simon.

'You must take after your father,' she said.

It was a throwaway comment, but Simon's face closed and his mouth set in a compressed line.

'No, I don't,' he said harshly. 'I don't resemble him at all.'

CHAPTER THREE

'Wow.' A-glitter with lights, London lay spread out below Simon's apartment. Across the Thames, the bridges were illuminated as if strung with fairy lights, and Clara could see right down to the Houses of Parliament and the huge circle of the London Eye. In the darkness, the streets seemed to be shimmering with energy.

'Wow,' she said again. 'What a fabulous view! It feels like you're on top of the world, doesn't it?'

She turned back to admire the rest of the apartment, which was stark and stylish, and somehow not at all what she had expected of someone as conventional as Simon Valentine. 'What an amazing place.'

Simon shrugged as he pocketed his car keys. 'It's a convenient location for the City, and these properties make sound investments.'

'Right,' said Clara, who had never invested in property in her life.

'I think it's *ghastly*!' said Frances. She had

changed and was looking remarkably relaxed and elegant for someone who had been mugged hours earlier. 'I keep telling him that he should at least put up some curtains.'

She looked around her disparagingly. 'Soulless is the only word for it. What this place needs is a woman's touch,' she said as Simon blew out an exasperated breath, having clearly heard it all before. 'Don't you agree, Clara?'

Clara thought of the cluttered flat she shared with Allegra. It was cosier than Simon's apartment, that was for sure, but she couldn't see Simon wanting cushions and throws and magazines scattered on the sofa. He wouldn't like cold mugs of tea left lying around, shoes discarded on the floor or bras and tights drying over the radiators. That coffee table would never be buried under nail polishes and phone chargers and old newspapers and empty crisp packets and menus from the Indian takeaway round the corner.

In fact, the woman's touch was probably the last thing Simon needed.

'It's very spacious,' she said diplomatically.

Frances sniffed. 'I don't know why he doesn't buy a nice house in Chelsea or somewhere. It would be so much nicer for me to visit.' She heaved an exaggerated sigh but, when Simon remained unmoved, turned back to Clara.

'Anyway, come and sit down.' Without giving Clara an opportunity to protest, she drew her over towards one of the cream sofas and spoke over her shoulder to her son.

'Darling, do get Clara a drink. You must be gasping for a G&T,' she told Clara. 'I know I am! Or I suppose Simon could make tea,' she added doubtfully.

'Mother—' Simon's teeth were audibly gritted '—Clara's anxious to get home. She might not want a drink.'

'Nonsense, of course she does. Don't you, Clara?'

Clara was torn. Simon was clearly desperate to get rid of her, but it had been a long day and now that Frances had mentioned gin…

'I'd love a gin and tonic,' she confessed.

'There you are!' Frances turned triumphantly to her son. 'And I'll have one too, darling, to keep her company.'

Simon sucked in a breath. 'Of course,' he said tightly and disappeared to what Clara presumed was a kitchen.

'Don't mind him,' Frances said with a sunny

smile. 'He likes to disapprove, but it's good for him to relax a bit. He works so hard, poor darling, and now he's on his own again...' She leant towards Clara confidentially. 'Well, I always thought Astrid was a bit of a cold fish, but at least she would make him go out.'

Clara was dying to gossip, but didn't think she ought to. She asked Frances how long she was visiting instead, and Frances chatted happily about herself until Simon reappeared with drinks.

'Now you must tell us all about you,' she insisted, and proceeded to grill Clara about her family, background and job.

'Oh, you work in television? How exciting! Simon's on television sometimes.'

Clara's eyes met Simon's fleetingly over the rim of her glass. 'Yes, I know.' She had to give him points for being able to pour a mean gin and tonic. It was long and fizzy, with just the right amount of lime and ice. She was feeling better already and she settled back into the sofa, prepared to enjoy herself before she had to face the reality of failure again.

'You must be very proud,' she said to Frances. 'Oh, I am, *terribly*. Of course, the idea of him being a pin-up is a bit of a hoot. Not that he wasn't a *gorgeous* baby.'

'*Mother...*'

Clara smothered a smile at Simon's expression as Frances rattled on. 'I see him on the news, and he sounds so clever and *sensible*. You'd never guess what a reckless little boy he was, would you?'

'Mother—' said Simon again, warning in his voice '—Clara's had a long day. She doesn't want to listen to a lot of boring family stories.'

Frances ignored him and spoke to a fascinated Clara. 'He was full of mischief when he was little. Your hair would stand on end if I told you half the things he got up to! But then his father died...' She trailed off sadly. 'That was a horrible shock. I don't know what I would have done without Simon then. He sorted everything out, and he's been looking after us ever since.'

Simon's jaw was set. 'That's not true—'

'It *is* true,' insisted Frances. 'I always wonder how different you'd have been if your father hadn't left things in such a mess.'

What mess? Clara wondered. It sounded as if there was an interesting story there, but when Simon caught her eye his expression was so tense that she couldn't help responding to his unspoken appeal.

'I really should be going,' she interrupted Frances, who was clearly ready to tell the whole story. Draining her glass, she put it down and, one-armed, manoeuvred herself awkwardly to her feet from the deep sofa.

'Must you go?' Frances looked disappointed. 'It's been such fun meeting you, and I'm so, *so* grateful to you.'

'It was nothing, really.'

'It wasn't nothing. You were an absolute *hero-ine*, and you've broken your wrist rescuing my wretched bag. I can't possibly thank you enough. You must *promise* to tell us if there's ever anything we can ever do for you. Mustn't she, Simon?'

A nerve jerked in Simon's cheek. 'Of course,' he said after the tiniest of hesitations.

'That's settled then.'

Frances fussed around, trying to remember where she'd put Clara's bag, while Clara and Simon waited in awkward silence. Eventually it was found, and Frances handed it over, kissed Clara on the cheek and made her promise to keep in touch.

At last she let them go, waving them off from the door of Simon's apartment.

He waited until the lift doors were closed before he spoke.

'Thank you,' he said gruffly.

Clara didn't pretend not to know what he was talking about. 'My mother can be really embarrassing, too.'

'Does she regale perfect strangers with stories of what you did as a little girl?' he asked, but his expression lightened a little.

'Not exactly. She and Dad are both academics, and my brothers are really clever too. They all listen to classical music and read highbrow novels and if they go to the theatre, it's to watch some avant-garde play, while I flick through magazines and love show tunes.' Clara sighed. 'My family are lovely, but sometimes I can feel them thinking that there must have been some mix-up at the hospital when I was born.'

'They don't sound too embarrassing,' said Simon.

'That's because you've got a PhD,' she pointed out. 'Try taking a boyfriend home.'

She had a momentary pang when she thought about Matt, who had done better than most at coping with her family. But then, of course, he would have done. Matt got on with everybody. Clara pushed the memory aside.

'He gets grilled on what he thinks about existentialist literature or Saint Augustine's theology, and if the poor guy is brave enough to ask a question of his own about what they do, he gets a whole lecture on the spatial politics of post Reformation churches.'

'The what?'

'I think it's something to do with kneeling,' said Clara. 'I ought to know. My mother's been writing a book about it since I was five. I used to envy my friends who had proper mothers who read *Glitz* and watched television and talked about make-up and celebrities. The only famous people Mum knows about have been dead four hundred years!'

'At least she doesn't keep running off and marrying unsuitable men,' said Simon as they headed back to the car.

'How many times has your mother been married?'

'Three, and every time she manages to pick someone who'll leave her high and dry.' Clara could hear the bitter undercurrent in his voice as he unlocked the car and helped her in so that she didn't jar her wrist. His hand, she noticed, was firm and his grip surprisingly strong.

'You'd think she would learn from experience, but no!' Simon said, unaware of the tiny and disturbing frisson shimmying its way down Clara's spine. 'She'll throw everything up for "love" and, before we know where we are, she's having to extricate herself from another mess.'

Or was he the one who had to extricate his mother every time? Clara wondered, glad to feel that the frisson had reached the coccyx and appeared to have vanished. Perhaps she had imagined it?

'I think it's nice that she hasn't lost her faith in love,' she said neutrally when Simon settled himself behind the steering wheel.

'She thinks she needs a husband, but that's not true. Mother likes to tell everyone that I looked after her when my father died, but that's not true. *She* was the one who kept us going, and it was hard for her. Whenever she's at her most exasperating—which is often—I remember that.'

'Is that why you won't do a programme about romance? Because it never worked out for your mother?'

'No,' said Simon with a withering look. 'I won't do it because (a), I'm extremely busy with more important things and (b), frankly the last thing I want at the moment is more media exposure. I didn't mind when I could draw attention to the micro-financing crisis, but nobody ever mentions that now, and instead I get sackloads of fan mail from silly women who have obviously got nothing better to do with their time. I wouldn't keep doing the news interviews at all if the CEO of Stanhope Harding hadn't insisted it was good PR.'

Clearly remembering that particular conversation, he shoved the car into gear with unnecessary force. 'He didn't quite tell me that my job depended on continuing to comment, but I got the message.'

'Mmm,' said Clara, unable to resist. 'It's hard, isn't it, when your job depends on your boss, who insists that you do something you don't particularly want to do.'

Simon said nothing, but the distinctly abrasive quality to the silence told her that he had got the point.

You must promise to tell us if there's ever anything we can ever do for you, Frances had said.

And then Simon had been forced to say, *Of course.*

He must know that there was indeed something he could do for her.

Apart from directions to the flat she shared in a shabby street in south-west London, the journey passed in silence. Clara folded her lips together and heroically refrained from reminding Simon of his mother's promise, but she knew that he was thinking about it. Whenever she sneaked a glance at him from under her lashes, she could see a muscle jerking in his jaw.

Miraculously, Simon managed to find a parking space only a little way down the street from Clara's flat. He switched off the engine, but neither of them moved.

The silence lengthened. His jaw was still working, Clara noted. It would be a mistake to say anything, but he could do with just a *tiny* push.

Lifting her arm in its sling, she winced. Not too much. Just enough to suggest great pain, bravely borne, but not so bravely that he didn't notice. It was a delicate balance.

'Oh, all *right*!' Simon ground out as if she had been nagging him for the entire journey.

Clara opened her eyes at him, all innocence. 'What?'

'I'll do your bloody programme, all right?' he snarled. 'There's no need to keep going *on* about it!'

'I didn't say a word,' protested Clara, careful to conceal her jubilance.

'You didn't need to. I know perfectly well you registered what my mother said. *You must promise to let us know if there's ever anything we can do for you,*' he mimicked Frances savagely. 'One of these days I'm going to wring her neck!'

'Oh, don't do that! She's so lovely.'

Far from agreeing, Simon blew out a breath and glowered through the windscreen. 'You'd better tell me what she's let me in for,' he said heavily.

'It won't be that bad, honestly.' Now that he was on the point of agreeing, Clara perversely began to feel a little sorry for him. 'We're not asking you to take part in any stunts or cheap tricks. Ted is a brilliant director. MediaOchre has won several awards for documentaries we've made, and we're expecting this one to be just as successful.'

She could hardly believe she was getting to do the speech she had practised so carefully at last. This was worth a broken wrist!

'*Romance: Fact or Fiction?* will be a serious examination of romance,' she assured him. 'We're going to look at what it is and how it works and why it's so popular around the world, but we want to get beyond the clichés.'

'Right.' Simon's voice dripped disbelief.

'Your presence will give the programme real gravitas,' Clara went on, ignoring his scepticism. 'Stella Holt is incredibly popular at the moment, so she'll represent the "romantic" idea while you would be in the "anti-romance" camp, if you like. I know Stella is very keen to work with you on this,' she added. 'We think the contrast between the two of you will make for intriguing television.'

'Intriguing television…ye gods.' Simon rubbed a hand over his face. 'I can't believe I'm even listening to this!'

Clearly she wasn't converting him to the idea. Clara ploughed on. 'The plan is to shoot the film in three classic "romantic" locations. One will be Paris, obviously.'

'I thought you were going to avoid clichés?'

'We're *testing* the clichés,' she said firmly. 'After Paris, we'll film on a tropical island and, for the last segment, Ted wants me to find somewhere wild and stormy—a cottage in the Highlands, for instance.' She looked at him hopefully. 'What do you think?'

'I think it's the most ridiculous idea I've ever heard,' said Simon, not mincing his words. 'What's it supposed to prove?'

'Well, for a start, we'll consider whether those places are romantic or not—will you feel more romantic when you're there, and do they make you behave differently?'

'I can tell you now that I won't,' he said, his mouth set in an implacable line. 'I don't do romance.'

'Then that's what you'll say.' Clara kept her voice calm. It was like dealing with a skittish horse. Having got this close, she didn't want to spook him now, before she'd slipped that bridle over his head and got him to finally agree. She was *almost* there. Already her fingers were itching to pull out her phone and call Ted with the news.

Simon sighed and rubbed his hand over his face again. Reluctance incarnate.

'So it would just be those three trips?'

'Three short trips, which we would accommodate to your schedule, of course. For you it'll mean free trips to Paris, the Indian Ocean and Scotland,' Clara added, still in economist whisperer mode. 'That can't be bad, can it?'

Oops, wrong thing to say. 'If there's one thing people need to understand about the economy, it's that there's no such thing as "free",' said Simon quellingly. 'Everything has to be paid for somewhere along the line.'

'I can assure you we wouldn't be asking you to pay anything.'

'I'd be paying with my professional reputation. And my time.'

Personally, Clara would have thought the chance to go to the tropical island of St Bonaventure alone was worth the trade, but she bit her lip on the comment.

'We'd make all the arrangements,' she said, trying another tack. 'You wouldn't have to do anything but turn up and do your piece to the camera.'

'And if I agree, will you shut up and leave me alone?'

'Absolutely.'

'No more phone calls, no more emails, no more throwing yourself at muggers?'

'Well, I'd need to get in touch with you about

travel arrangements, but other than that, you won't even know I exist,' promised Clara.

Simon thought that was deeply unlikely. Once you knew Clara Sterne existed, it would be very hard to forget her. There weren't that many people who would tackle a mugger to save a stranger's bag. She sat there, shimmering with energy, brimming with colour even in the dim light, her eyes fixed expectantly on his face.

God only knew what he had got himself into! But now that she had explained the deal, perhaps it wouldn't be *quite* as bad as he'd imagined. It might even be possible to salvage something from the whole mess.

'You mentioned a follow-up programme on the micro-financed projects,' he reminded Clara.

'Er…yes, I did, didn't I?'

Simon was fairly sure Clara didn't have the authority to agree which programmes the company would make, but if MediaOchre wanted him badly enough, he might have some leverage to get the follow-ups made. It would be good for the projects and keep the issue alive in the fickle media.

'Can you guarantee that will be your next project?' he pressed her.

'I can say we'll do our very best to get it commissioned,' she said and he could practically see her crossing her fingers.

'All right,' he said, resigned, 'in that case, you can tell your boss I'll do it and you get to keep your job.'

Her face lit up with a smile, and for the strangest moment Simon had the dazzling sensation that the car had filled with sunshine. 'Oh, *thank* you!' she said. 'Thank you, thank you, thank you! You won't regret it, I promise you. It's going to be fantastic!'

Simon doubted that too, but he got out to open her door, take her bag and help her out. It wasn't that easy one-armed, and he saw her wince as she knocked the plaster on the door frame. A real wince, not that fake remember-what-your-mother-promised wince she had done earlier.

A slight frown touched his eyes. 'Are you going to be all right?'

'Oh, I'll be fine,' she said buoyantly, glancing along at the house, where lamps were lit in the window of what was obviously an upstairs flat. 'It looks like Allegra is home, so she can let me in.'

She hoisted her bag onto her good shoulder and

beamed at him. 'Thank you again, Simon. I'll be in touch.'

One hand on the open door of the car, Simon watched her literally dancing down the pavement. She had her phone to her ear already. 'Ted!' he heard her say joyfully. 'He's agreed! It's going to be all right! Everything's perfect.'

The concourse at St Pancras was crowded. Simon checked his watch, and then the name of the coffee bar behind him again. He had agreed to meet Clara there ten minutes ago.

He was in no mood for a so-called romantic trip to Paris. His last hope, that the CEO of Stanhope Harding would refuse permission for him to take the time off had been quashed when the board had decided that in the current economic climate it would be politic to show the 'friendly face' of financial services.

One more disaster to chalk up to the banking crisis, in fact.

And as if it wasn't bad enough being roped into this charade—a programme about romance, for God's sake!—a signal failure on the Circle line had meant that he was five minutes late, and

Simon hated unpunctuality. It smacked too much of a lack of control.

He hadn't been looking forward to apologising to Clara, but there had been no sign of her when he'd arrived, and that made him even crosser.

Surely she could have made an effort to be there on time after all the fuss she had made about getting him to agree to take part in her ridiculous programme? Simon was bitterly regretting having succumbed to that martyred little wince.

This was all his mother's fault! If she hadn't carried a ridiculous handbag just begging to be snatched by a mugger, Clara would never have broken her wrist and he would have felt under no obligation whatsoever.

Simon eyed the passing crowd morosely. It was coming up for Valentine's Day. February was never a good time to be burdened with his surname. Why couldn't his ancestors have chosen a decent Anglo-Saxon name like Smith or Brown? The shop windows were plastered with red hearts, and the concourse was full of loved-up couples wandering hand in hand. They were probably all going to Paris for a romantic weekend too, as if this trip wasn't going to be excruciating enough.

Where was Clara? Frowning, he looked at his

watch again. True to her word, she had restricted herself to contacting him about practical arrangements, and had proved surprisingly efficient. Until now, anyway. Offered the choice between flying and taking the train, Simon had opted for Eurostar, which was quicker and more convenient than hanging around airports. He had his laptop with him and could work more effectively on the train.

If Clara ever turned up with the tickets.

A few yards away a crowd had gathered. They were all watching something, and laughing and cheering. Simon took a few steps closer to see what they were all so damned happy about.

Craning his neck, he was able to see round two women talking volubly in French, and his astonished gaze fell on Clara. Dressed in a denim jacket, a red jumper and a short skirt, with the same vividly striped scarf wound carelessly several times around her throat, she was performing a tap dance routine to much encouragement and applause from her audience. From the elbow downwards, her arm was encased in a lime-green cast, but it didn't seem to be bothering her at all. Her cheeks were pink and her hair swung wildly around her face, while her skirt swished, revealing long legs clad in diamond-patterned tights.

She was laughing, responding to the crowd, but when her gaze met his with an almost audible clash, her feet faltered and she stopped in dismay.

'Omigod!' she said, clapping a hand to her forehead. 'What time is it?'

As one, the crowd turned to stare at Simon, making him feel like a monster for interrupting their entertainment.

'Twenty past,' he said.

'I am *so* sorry.' Clara grabbed her bag, waved a general farewell with her lime-green cast, and pushed through her admirers towards him. 'I was here on time, honestly I was, but there was this little girl who was so miserable,' she explained breathlessly. 'Her mother said she had a bad ear and they were going home without seeing *Cats*, which they'd come specially to London to see, so I just did a little routine from the show to entertain her, and suddenly there were all these people watching, and I forgot the time, I'm afraid. I always wanted to be Ginger Rogers...'

She trailed off at the unresponsive look on Simon's face. 'Sorry, I get a bit carried away when I dance, and it's not often I get an audience.' She was digging around in her bag for the tickets with her good hand. 'I don't suppose *you* dance?'

'Do I look like Fred Astaire to you?'

Clara stopped, her hand still buried in her bag, and studied him. Simon Valentine had dressed for a romantic weekend in Paris in a suit, with a pale blue shirt and a darker blue tie with some kind of crest on it. He had a laptop case in one hand and an overnight bag in the other, both black and no-nonsense, and his expression was distant.

No, not a man about to burst into song or twirl her around the concourse.

'Not really,' she said. 'But I'm always ready to be surprised.'

'I'm afraid what you see is what you get,' said Simon, and she sighed.

'I thought that might be the case.'

Clara had arranged a Business Premier ticket for Simon, and Roland had grudgingly agreed that she could travel in the same class. Which was big of him, given that she had spent the past three weeks setting up deals with airlines and hotels and saving him thousands of pounds on the budget.

It had been a frantic time to get it all organised, and Clara was looking forward to travelling in comfort. She accepted the glass of champagne that was offered as soon as they boarded with the aplomb of one born to travel first class, as opposed to one who spent most of her time on buses or battling the rush hour on the underground. This was the life! Settling into her seat, she looked around appreciatively.

'This is exciting, isn't it?'

She beamed at Simon, who had taken a glass of water instead of champagne and was opening his computer.

'Thrilling.'

Clara tutted at his deadpan tone. 'Can you really say you don't feel even a tiny frisson at the idea of going to Paris for a weekend?' she asked as she attempted to unwind her scarf one-handed.

'I don't even know what a frisson is,' said Simon as his laptop whirred and bleeped into life.

'And then you wonder that your girlfriend dumped you for an Italian hottie!' Clara grimaced as her scarf got caught behind her, and she tugged at it fruitlessly until Simon sucked in an exasperated breath and got up to help her.

'Stand up,' he ordered, and Clara wriggled obediently out of her seat. She stood very still as he disentangled her briskly. Her eyes were fixed above his collar where his throat met his jaw, and for some reason her heart started to thud against her ribs. All at once he seemed very solid and very male.

He smelled nice too, and she wondered what it would be like to lean forward and press her lips to his skin.

The thought veered out of nowhere and caught Clara unawares, so much like a blow to the stomach driving all the air from her lungs that she actually flinched.

'What?' said Simon.

'Nothing.' Clara bundled the scarf up in her hands. 'Thanks,' she said, avoiding his eyes and slipping back into her seat. Her heart was still pattering ridiculously, and she found that she was breathing very carefully.

At least Simon didn't appear to have noticed anything. He sat down, produced a pair of horn-rimmed spectacles and put them on before turning his attention to the computer screen.

Clara studied him covertly. It wasn't that he was *un*attractive, but he was so stern, so conventional. Nothing there to make her heart hammer in her throat, or the breath leak out of her lungs.

'Did you ever take Astrid to Paris for a romantic

weekend?' she asked the moment her breathing had settled, just to prove that it had been a momentary aberration.

Simon didn't even look up from the screen. 'We didn't have that kind of relationship,' he said stiffly.

'What kind of relationship *did* you have?'

'A good one,' he said, but this time he did meet her gaze over the laptop. 'It worked very well. We both had our own space. We *agreed*.' A faint defensive edge had crept into his voice. 'It was what we both wanted. No complicated emotions.'

Clara considered that. 'It doesn't sound like much fun.'

'It wasn't about fun. It was about companionship…mutual satisfaction.'

Sex, presumably. Clara chose not to examine why the idea of that should leave her feeling nettled.

'So what happened if it was so satisfying for both of you?'

At first she thought Simon wasn't going to answer. He pressed a key and watched something appear on the screen. 'Paolo was at some reception we both went to. God knows how he got in! He doesn't have a clue about finance. He's something to do with fashion.' Simon said it as if it were a dirty word. 'Apparently he sent Astrid roses the next day, and begged to meet her again. She said she'd been swept off her feet.'

He looked so baffled by the idea that Clara felt quite sorry for him.

'It sounds like she wanted some romance, and she wasn't getting any from you.'

'She said she didn't want any of that nonsense!'

'She might have said that, but when she found out what it could be like, she obviously changed her mind.'

Clara put down her champagne and leant forward. She was feeling herself again, thank goodness. 'You know, I think making this programme will be good for you, Simon. You should be able to pick up all sorts of little hints this weekend, and then put them into action when you get home.'

Simon had been running his finger over the mouse pad, but he glanced up at that, his brows drawn together. 'Hints?'

'If you want Astrid back, that is. Paolo might have swept her off her feet, but you could always sweep her back now that you know that she likes some romance. You could organise a lovely weekend for her in Paris. I'm sure she'd love the hotel where we're staying, for instance,' said Clara, warming to her theme. 'You could arrange for champagne and flowers in the room and then take her out to dinner. I've researched the perfect romantic restaurant, and the best place for dancing...'

Picking up her glass once more, she sighed a little wistfully and sipped her champagne. 'I'd love it if someone did that for me!'

'So why isn't your boyfriend taking *you* to Paris this weekend?' said Simon nastily.

There was a tiny pause. 'Mainly because he married his childhood sweetheart and they're expecting their first baby any day now.'

Clara smiled hard to show Simon that she was perfectly fine about it.

'Ah,' said Simon.

CHAPTER FOUR

AWARE that the tables had turned, and that it wasn't that comfortable to be quizzed about your failed relationship, Clara fiddled with the cast on her hand as she looked out of the window. Simon had told her about Astrid, so it was only fair that she told him her own story.

'Matt was very romantic. He took me to Seville for my birthday two years ago. It was perfect. He was everything I'd ever wanted,' she remembered. 'I was sure he was The One, and that we'd be together for ever. I was *so* happy.'

Simon didn't say anything but, when she glanced back, she saw that he was watching her rather than his computer screen, so she went on.

'I thought he was going to ask me to marry him while we were in Seville, but he didn't. So I thought maybe he would do it when we got home, and when he sat me down and said he wanted to talk to me, I was so excited I couldn't really take in what he was saying at first.'

Her mouth twisted a little at the memory. 'And when I *did* take it in, I couldn't believe it. He told me that he'd met Sophie again a couple of weeks before, and that they'd realised that they were meant to be together. It turned out that I was just a rebound relationship.'

Simon would never have made an agony aunt. Clara could tell that she was making him uneasy. Now, if only she could talk to him about the derivatives market or public sector debt, he might be some use. Still, he was listening, even if it clearly terrified him that she was about to cry or do something equally alarming and emotional.

Which she wasn't. Clara put a bright smile back in place just to prove it.

She didn't do crying. She did singing, dancing, joking. She did anything that would stop her thinking about how much it had hurt when Matt had left, about the rawness of her heart and the loneliness she tucked away deep inside her.

'Why did he bother taking you to Seville if he was going to end things as soon as you got home?' Simon asked after a moment.

'He didn't want to spoil my birthday,' she said. Even now, the memory of that awful evening made her wince. 'He was being kind. He did really like me, he said. If it hadn't been for Sophie, we could have been happy together, he said. It was just that as soon as he'd seen her again, he'd known that he loved her still. Sophie was the love of his life, he said, but he wanted us to stay friends.'

'And are you friends?'

'Oh, well, you know how it is,' said Clara, super-casual. 'Life's just one hectic social whirl. There's television to be watched and analysed in depth, nails to be painted, magazines to be read… Allegra and I have to keep up to date with all the latest fashion disasters and celebrity news. It's a wonder we have time for work at all!'

'I take it that's a no,' said Simon sardonically.

'We're not *not* friends,' she said. 'It's just that our lives have gone in different directions.'

Matt had married Sophie and was blissfully happy, and she had been left on her own.

'We keep in touch,' she added, very slightly on the defensive. 'I know about the baby. And I'm glad for him.'

She *was*.

'There would have been no point in us staying together if he was in love with someone else,'

Clara said, just as she'd said to herself so many times. 'We'd have both been miserable.'

'You seem happy now,' said Simon after a moment.

'I've got a lot to be happy about.' Clara drained her champagne with a sort of defiance and set the glass back down on the table between them with a click. 'I've got my family, I've got friends. I've somewhere to live and a job I love.

'Actually, it was the job that made the most difference to me,' she told Simon. 'I'd never had a career before. I used to dream about starring in a musical, maybe going to Broadway, but I wasn't dedicated enough, and the truth is that I wasn't good enough either. I did a couple of tours with a third-rate company, and got the occasional job doing ads, but it wasn't exactly starry stuff, and even that dried up and I had to keep myself going by waitressing and temping. So when Matt left me I fell apart, and it felt as if I had nothing. It was Ted who saved me.'

'Ted?'

'You'll meet him in Paris. He's the director, and brilliant at it too. He also happens to be one of my best friends. I was an absolute mess, but Ted mopped me up, and when MediaOchre

Productions had a vacancy for a research assistant he bullied me into applying for it. He said it was time I tried a proper job, and the fact is I've loved working there. I'm much better at making arrangements and pulling together all the loose ends on a project than I am at dancing.'

'I'm glad to hear it,' said Simon dryly, clearly thinking about her performance at St Pancras.

Clara ignored that. 'I'm a production assistant now, and I want to be a producer, and eventually work in drama. That's my dream, anyway,' she confessed.

It was a dream that kept her going, and filled the awful gap Matt had left in her life.

'Roland Richards—he's executive producer and owns MediaOchre—promised me a shot at producing a programme if we could get *Romance: Fact or Fiction?* made.'

'Oh, so that's why you kept hassling me?'

'Well, yes.' Clara looked contrite. 'But I do really think it'll be a great programme,' she added hastily. 'It's just that I love this job, and I've never made a success of anything before now. I can't imagine feeling for anybody else what I felt for Matt, so I'm determined to focus on my career now, and this programme is part of that and a step towards what I really want to do.'

'It's unwise to invest emotion in a job,' said Simon disapprovingly. 'It's not logical.'

'Not everything can be decided by logic,' Clara protested.

'It would be a lot better if everything was,' said Simon. 'As soon as people start substituting emotion for clear thinking, that's when things go wrong. It all gets muddled and messy. If everyone understood that all relationships are at heart economic ones, there would be a lot less agonising.'

'That's rubbish!' said Clara. 'You can't reduce love to economics.'

'You can dress it up all you like in hearts and flowers, but the reality is that economic imperatives drive the way we think, the way we behave, and the way we feel.'

Simon leant back and regarded Clara over the rim of his glasses. 'Take you and this job that you "love". You wouldn't do it if it didn't give you an income that means you can pay for the basic necessities of food and shelter, would you?'

'I have to earn my living, sure, but that doesn't mean I don't love what I do,' she objected.

'What exactly do you "love" about it?'

'Well, there's the opportunity to meet charmers like you,' said Clara sarcastically before she could help herself.

'But you only want me because you need my cooperation to get the programme made and, if I've understood the situation correctly, if you don't get the programme made, the future of MediaOchre Productions is at risk. No MediaOchre Productions means no job for you, no matter how much you love it, which means no income, which means you'll be struggling for your essentials again. So we're back to economics.'

'So what are you saying? I'm not allowed to enjoy my job?'

'Not at all. I'm saying when you talk about having a dream, you should ground it in economic reality, not in waffly concepts like "loving" what you do.'

'Well.' Clara felt quite huffy. 'So what's your dream? Or is dreaming too illogical for you?'

'Dream is a very emotive word. I've got goals and ambitions, certainly.'

'Like what?'

Simon eyed Clara across the table. She had shrugged off her jacket and, above the red jumper, her eyes looked bright and brown, like a robin's.

All at once he found himself remembering the softness of her scarf as he unwound it, the downward sweep of her lashes, the fresh fragrance that drifted up from her hair.

Things he didn't usually notice at all.

It was odd. Taken feature by feature, she wasn't particularly pretty, but there was a quirkiness about her that was quite appealing, he supposed. She was nowhere near as lovely as Astrid, of course. Astrid was coolly elegant, even serene—except when she was being swept off her feet by passionate Italians—while Clara was all colour and movement. Astrid would never have made an exhibition of herself in the middle of the station concourse, that was for sure.

Clara reminded Simon uneasily of his mother, who had the same impulsiveness, who gave exactly the same impression of being on the verge of doing something crazily illogical. Even Clara's face was full of movement. The edges of her mouth, her cheekbones, her lashes, even the corners of her eyes seemed to be tilting very slightly upwards, as if she were on the point of breaking into a smile. It annoyed Simon that he kept watching her, waiting for it to happen.

Not that there was much sign of her smiling

right then. She was leaning forward, her expression combative, as she waited for him to answer her question.

'What *are* your goals?' she insisted.

That was easy. 'I want people to understand the economic forces that shape their lives. I want them to have access to financial systems that help them to help themselves,' he said. 'That's what the micro-finance projects are all about.'

'But that's general,' Clara objected. 'I was thinking about personal goals. What do you want for *yourself*?'

Simon adjusted his glasses, annoyed to find that he had to think about it.

'Financial security,' he said.

'That's it?' She stared at him. 'Not love? Not happiness?'

'Security is the basis of everything else,' said Simon. 'That's enough for me.'

Pointedly, Simon turned his attention back to his computer, and to his relief she fell silent. He allowed himself to hope that she'd lost interest, and made a show of looking up the markets, but the truth was that he was unsettlingly aware of her still. There was a warmth and vibrancy to Clara that made the very air around her shimmer.

He frowned at the thought. It wasn't like him to be so fanciful. He ought to be able to ignore her easily. If only she didn't ask such awkward questions! Now, instead of focusing on his laptop, he was thinking about what he really wanted, and what was the point of that?

Simon had never doubted it before. Ever since his father's death, he had preferred figures to people. Figures made sense. They stayed still so that you could grasp them. They didn't veer off course illogically, or plunge from one ridiculous situation to the next the way his mother did. They weren't reckless or disturbing. They were *safe*.

Astrid had made him feel like that. She wasn't alarming or demanding. She never insisted on talking about their relationship or knowing what he was feeling. She never wittered on about goals or looked at him as if he were somehow deficient for not wanting to take risks.

Perhaps it wasn't a very exciting goal to stay as you were, Simon thought, vaguely defensive, but once you had what you wanted, once you had everything under control and no one could throw your world upside down, why keep on striving for more?

* * *

It was pouring when they arrived in Paris. Ted was there already, with Steve the cameraman and Peter on sound. 'They're doing establishing shots,' Clara told Simon in the taxi to the hotel.

'What the hell is an establishing shot?' Simon was still in a bad mood. He had made it clear that he wanted to work but, instead of sitting and reading quietly, or working herself as Astrid would have done, Clara had left him to it, and gone wandering off. Before he knew what had happened, she was sharing another glass of champagne with an American couple and a businessman from Lyons, and they were all getting on like a proverbial fire in a match factory.

They were too far away for Simon to hear their conversation, so he couldn't even complain that they were disturbing him, but he was aware of them laughing all the same. It was obvious that Clara was having a great time, and was clearly not the slightest bit bothered that he was too busy to talk. All in all, he hadn't managed any work at all, and now it was raining!

The entire trip was turning out to be a disaster, he thought grouchily.

Clara was explaining about establishing shots, as if he really cared. 'They're location shots,' she said. 'You know, the Eiffel Tower, to signal to the viewer that we're in Paris and general views to give a sense of place. I had a message from Ted, who said the weather wasn't too bad this morning, so they'll be glad they came early.'

She looked eagerly through the taxi window, apparently unfazed by his unresponsive mood. 'It's great to be here at last! Now we just need Stella. She said she wanted to fly, so Roland's accompanying her. They should be arriving later and you'll have a chance to meet her before we start shooting tomorrow.'

'So why are we here so early?' Simon asked grumpily.

'You said you wanted to work on the train,' she reminded him. 'There's plenty to do. I've got to check the equipment, and block out some scenes with you and Ted.'

'What scenes?' he asked in alarm.

'Nothing is rehearsed, but obviously we need an idea of what you and Stella are going to say,' Clara said patiently. 'I'll just list some bullet points for you to cover when you're talking. We'll need to recce some special locations. I've done quite a lot of research, but you never really know how good a place is going to look on camera until you actually get there. I can't wait to see the hotel,' she added, craning her head as if she could get the taxi to move faster through the heavy traffic on the *périphérique*. 'It sounds fab.'

Fab wasn't a word Simon would ever have used, but even he had to admit that it was a very attractive hotel, tucked into a quiet street near the Luxembourg Gardens. The taxi dropped them by a heavy Parisian door, and they stepped through into a hidden cobbled courtyard and another world.

Inside, the hotel was chic and charming, and it reeked of expense down to the last light switch. A hush of wealth hung over the reception, where Clara managed to look utterly out of place and yet completely at ease.

'I thought MediaOchre were tottering on the brink of bankruptcy,' Simon muttered out of the corner of his mouth as he waited with Clara for the lift. 'How on earth did you afford a place like this?'

'I negotiated a deal,' Clara whispered back. 'There will just happen to be a couple of shots of the hotel in the final edit. You'd be surprised what we can get in return for a bit of free publicity.'

To Simon's critical eyes, the room was over-decorated, with a flounce too many around the bed, but Clara was thrilled with it. 'Oh, isn't it *gorgeous*?' she said, opening the bathroom and oohing and aahing at the polished taps, fluffy towels and free toiletries.

Careless of the rain, she threw open the French windows and stepped out onto the tiny balcony. 'Look, you can see the Eiffel Tower from here!'

Her face was alight as she turned back to Simon, wiping the raindrops from her cheeks, and he was alarmed to feel an odd little clutch in the area of his heart.

'Oh, this is perfect!' she said, waving the lime-green cast around. 'I'm so excited! You can't get more romantic than this, can you?'

It was just a room to Simon, but he was reluctant to burst her bubble. 'I'm glad you like it,' he said gruffly. 'Well, if you tell me where my room is, I'll go and get settled.'

Clara laughed. 'This *is* your room! You don't think they put the crew in rooms like this, do you? I negotiated three lovely rooms for you, Stella and Roland, but the rest of us are in rooms at the back.'

'That's not very fair,' said Simon, frowning, but Clara shrugged.

'It's how it is. We're lucky we're in the same hotel. Often the talent get a smart hotel, while the rest of us are in some grotty place round the corner.'

'The talent?'

'That's you, in this case,' she said with a grin. 'You and Stella.'

He made a face. 'Look, why don't we swap rooms?' he heard himself suggesting.

'Swap?' Clara stared at him, and Simon gestured around the room.

'It's just somewhere to sleep to me. I don't care what the décor is like or how fluffy my pillows are. It sounded to me as if you would really enjoy sleeping here.'

'Of course I would, but—'

'I don't care where I sleep,' he added irritably.

She looked at him closely, as if to check that he wasn't joking. 'That's really generous of you,' she said, still uncertain, 'but I've hired a whole lot of equipment, and anything Ted isn't using at the moment will be in my room so that I can check it tonight.'

'Get it moved here.'

'Simon, I can't…' Clara protested, half laughing. 'You're one of the presenters. I can't put you in a poky room at the back!'

'You're not putting me anywhere. I've made the decision.'

Unsure quite why he was making such an issue of it, Simon scowled and stomped over to the door. 'A room like this is wasted on me. I saw the rates downstairs and, no matter how good a deal you got, you're still paying a lot of money for somewhere to sleep. That's only worth it if the room is used by someone who will appreciate it, and I won't. It's exactly the kind of bad economic practice that I find offensive,' he added austerely. 'Squandering money for the sake of it… I refuse to be part of it,' he said, ending the discussion.

'Roland would have a fit,' said Clara, but he could tell she was tempted.

'Tell him I insisted.'

Brushing her attempts to protest aside, he dragged her back to Reception and made her switch their rooms. A bellboy was despatched with a trolley to transfer all the camera and sound equipment to the room at the front, while Clara and Simon went back to retrieve his case.

'I don't know what to say.' Clara looked around

her a little helplessly. 'I can't believe I'll really get to sleep in a room like this! Thank you,' she said, smiling at him. 'It's beautiful.'

When Simon saw the room that Clara had been expected to share with a great pile of kit, he was quite cross. Barely more than a cupboard, it was adequate for his own needs, of course, but she would have been really uncomfortable.

He tossed his bag on the bed, and opened his laptop on the desk. They had agreed to meet a couple of hours later, but for now he was alone and could get on with some work. At last!

Rolling up his sleeves, Simon settled down at his computer, but the figures on the screen kept wavering as Clara's smile shimmered before his eyes instead. It was exasperating. There he was, trying to work, and all he could see was Clara, turning around, all bright red sweater and lime-green cast and long legs, smiling at him. *Thank you. It's beautiful.*

There was absolutely no reason for her smile to make him feel that good.

No reason for his chest to tighten.

No reason for him not to focus on work.

None at all.

* * *

In the end, Simon gave up and went down early to the chic lobby, where he sat on possibly the most uncomfortable chair he had ever tried and tried to focus on the *Financial Times*. Clara breezed in a few minutes later, brandishing an old-fashioned umbrella.

'Look what they gave me in Reception!' she said. 'It's going to be perfect!'

'Perfect?' Simon got to his feet and looked out through the doors, to where the rain was falling like stair rods into the courtyard. 'Clara, have you seen the weather? It's hard to imagine anything *less* perfect!'

But Clara refused to be daunted. 'What could be more romantic than sharing an umbrella as you wander around Paris? Maybe we'll get you and Stella to have a discussion under an umbrella,' she said excitedly.

'It won't be much of a discussion if no one can hear anything except the rain crashing onto the umbrella,' Simon pointed out and she waved her plaster cast to dismiss the problem.

'Details, details. The sound guy can work all that out.'

Swinging the umbrella in her good hand, she offered him a sunny smile quite at odds with the weather. 'Now, let's go and find us some romantic locations!'

She sounded so jaunty that Simon eyed the swinging umbrella with foreboding. 'Please tell me you're not going to start singing in the rain!'

Even he had heard of that song.

'It's funny you should mention that.' Clara sent him a wicked smile. 'It's one of my favourite routines.' And before Simon could stop her she was tap dancing around the umbrella and humming loudly while assorted well-dressed guests turned to stare.

'For God's sake, everybody's looking!' Simon scowled and snatched the umbrella back. 'I'm keeping this!'

Taking her by the arm, he propelled her towards the entrance. A doorman leapt to open the doors for them, and Simon let Clara go so that he could put up the umbrella with a snap.

'I forgot for a moment there what an exhibitionist you are!'

Clara wasn't in the least chastened. 'I just love to dance when I'm happy.'

'What is there to be happy about?' he grumbled as they picked their way through the puddles.

'Oh, it's not so bad, is it?'

'Clara, it's tipping it down! My shoes are soaked already. If you're trying to convince me that this is romantic, you're going the wrong way about it.'

'Wait till we're in Montmartre,' said Clara. 'Even you will have to admit it's romantic then!'

She made him climb all the way up the hill to the great white basilica of Sacré-Coeur. Simon was prepared to admit that the narrow streets would have been picturesque if they had been able to see much beyond the confines of the umbrella, and the view from the top probably was impressive if only it hadn't been obscured by sheets of rain.

He had been to Paris before, of course, but only to meetings in the financial district. Even if he had had the time, Montmartre's bohemian charm and street painters wouldn't have appealed. Perhaps because of the rain, it wasn't quite as touristy as he had feared. It felt as if they had the *quartier* to themselves. Everyone else was sensibly inside.

Only Clara would think of going out in this weather, he thought, exasperated. She was relentlessly upbeat about it, too, her face animated as she wittered on about mood and atmosphere and what she persisted in calling 'the romance of it all', while the neon-green cast swept through the gloomy light.

'Remind me again why this is romantic,' sighed Simon. They were standing under the umbrella in front of Sacré-Coeur, peering out over the terraced gardens to where Paris was lost in the murk. The rain drummed on the plastic over their heads, and splashed into the puddles. The bottom of Simon's trousers were soaked to the knees, and as for his shoes…!

Worst of all was being so aware of Clara beside him, exuding a warmth and vitality that banished the cold and the wet and the greyness beyond the shelter of the umbrella. They had to stand close together to keep out of the rain, and the shininess of her hair kept catching at the edge of his eye. Simon could smell it, a fresh, flowery fragrance that made him think of hot summer nights, which was odd when it was hard to imagine a more miserable February day.

It irritated Simon that he was finding it so hard to concentrate, especially when Clara herself didn't seem at all bothered by how close they were standing.

'I fail to see what's romantic about wet feet,' he added crossly.

'All right, it might not be romantic for us, but if we were lovers, you wouldn't be thinking about your feet,' said Clara, who hadn't been thinking about hers since they left the hotel. She had been too busy thinking about how much bigger Simon was when you were standing right next to him, how much more solid and steadying. How safe it felt to be with him.

It was weird now to remember how boring she had thought him at first. There was something about him that grew on you, Clara had decided. Simon was never going to be gorgeous, of course, but once you had started noticing the cool line of his mouth, or the firm angle of his jaw, you kept *on* noticing.

In fact, Clara wished that she could stop finding little details that made him, if not exactly hot, at least more attractive than expected: the squareness of his hands, the set of his shoulders, the creases at the edges of his eyes. There was a bit beneath his ear where his jaw met his throat, and every time Clara looked at it she felt a slow, disturbing thump that started low in her belly and muddled up her breathing.

The way it was doing then.

Simon was still grouchy. 'It would take a lot to make me forget about my feet right now,' he said.

'That's because you don't get romance.' Clara forced herself to sound bright and breezy, and not as if the blood was thudding along her veins and booming in her ears. 'If you were a romantic, it would be enough for you to be alone with your lover.'

She dragged her eyes from his throat and gestured at the umbrella above them. 'I mean, what could be more intimate? Just two of you under an umbrella, cut off from the rest of the world by the rain. You wouldn't care about how wet your feet were then. You'd just care that you were alone.'

Her expression grew misty. 'And when you kissed, the rain would disappear and you'd forget about your feet…'

'Then let's try it,' said Simon.

'Try what?' said Clara, who was still caught up in her imagined scene. She could picture it perfectly. The two lovers, the rain, the passion… She should be producing romantic films, not documentaries.

'A kiss.'

Clara snapped back to attention. *'What?'*

'I'm prepared to try anything to forget about my

wet feet,' he said, straight-faced, and she smiled uncertainly.

'You're not serious?'

'Why not? You keep telling me this is all romantic. I thought you could demonstrate.'

'But you don't want to kiss me!' Clara objected, still unable to decide whether he was joking or not.

'I thought *you* could kiss *me*,' said Simon. 'I'm prepared to be persuaded that there's something romantic about this situation,' he added, looking down at his sodden shoes, 'although I've got to say I'm not convinced so far!'

His gaze came back to Clara's doubtful face and he raised his brows. 'No? Fair enough. I suppose it's not *that* romantic, but if nothing else I thought it would take my mind off my feet.'

'Oh, I expect I could do that,' said Clara with an assumption of nonchalance that covered a pounding pulse and a mouth that was suddenly dry.

And the alarming knowledge that there was nothing she would like more than to kiss him.

'You're the talent, after all,' she said, 'and Roland would expect me to do whatever it took to keep you happy, even if it's just distracting you from your wet feet!'

That was it, she congratulated herself. Make a joke of it. She was good at that. And really, what was the problem? It would only be a kiss. She had been an actor, hadn't she? Kissing was just part of the job at times.

Besides, she might not get a better chance to convince Simon that there *was* such a thing as romance. He was so determinedly pragmatic about everything. Surely even *he* couldn't kiss pragmatically?

She would show him what a kiss could do, thought Clara, on her mettle. Simon might not want to admit that romance existed, but she would show him. She would pretend that he was Matt and give him a kiss he would never forget!

Lifting her chin, she turned to face him and stepped a little closer. It didn't take much to rest her palms flat against his chest. His body was broad and solid beneath the black coat.

Clara studied the raindrops spangled on the wool before she raised her eyes to Simon's. He was watching her steadily, his expression indecipherable.

'We have to imagine that we're in love,' she said as she slid her hands up to his shoulders.

Simon's expression didn't change, but Clara

could see a muscle jumping in his cheek. It made her think that he might not be *quite* as cool as he seemed, and her confidence grew.

'Whatever *that* means,' he said.

'It means that when we're together, we don't need anybody else,' said Clara, letting herself remember how she had felt when she was with Matt. 'It means that all we want is to be together, and to be able to touch each other.' Her palms smoothed thoughtfully around the collar of his coat. 'We can't keep our hands off each other, in fact. We don't care who might be watching.'

'Nobody is going to be watching in this rain,' Simon pointed out, but that telltale muscle in his cheek was still twitching.

'We don't even notice the rain when we're together,' Clara told him firmly.

'Why are we bothering with an umbrella in that case?'

'Don't be difficult,' she said, folding her lips together to stop herself laughing. She wasn't supposed to be laughing! But perversely it was easier now that she had remembered what she was doing. She had forgotten to be sad about Matt, and could tell herself that she was just trying to convince Simon of the power of romance.

Lowering her voice until it was suitably husky, she murmured, 'We're so in love that we don't care about anything but how right it feels when I kiss your throat like this...'

She touched her mouth to that tantalising place beneath his ear, and tried not to notice how good it *did* feel. His skin smelt wonderful: clean, crisp, male.

'If we were in love, you'd like it when I did that,' she told him.

'Maybe I like it anyway.' Simon's voice had deepened too. Clara could feel it reverberating through her, and she smiled.

'And this?' she asked, pressing little kisses along his jaw to the corner of his mouth.

'That too.'

'Then maybe you're getting the idea,' she said.

CHAPTER FIVE

THE rain beat down around them but beneath the umbrella it felt as if they were in a cocoon. Angling her mouth more comfortably, Clara pressed her lips against the firm warmth of his, and she felt him smile a little.

Simon Valentine, smiling. Who would have thought it? Heat fluttered through her, snaring the breath in her throat.

'How are those feet?' she asked, her voice not as steady as she would have liked.

'What feet?'

She laughed breathlessly, and Simon's arm came round her to pull her closer, while the hand holding the umbrella lowered until it was almost touching their heads.

Then *he* kissed *her*.

Well.

Well. Who would have thought that a stuffed shirt like Simon Valentine could kiss like *that*?

Clara was gripped by a strange giddy feeling.

She forgot that she was supposed to be proving a point. She forgot the programme. She forgot everything but the warmth of Simon's skin and the comforting solidity of his body as she leant against it.

Kissing him felt wonderful. His lips were so sure, and his arm around her so solid. It felt so good, in fact, that Clara was aware of a momentary disquiet. It was enough to make her consider drawing back before the kiss went any further, but the bit of her brain that thought that was a good idea didn't stand a chance against the whoosh of response that ignited deep inside her, that pressed her tighter against him and sent her arms winding round his neck as if of their own accord.

Perhaps it would have been sensible to stop then, but Clara had never been one to choose the sensible option when there was a reckless, exciting one on offer. She gave herself up to the kiss, to the sheer pleasure of it, as it grew deeper and hungrier and more urgent.

Clara never knew how long they would have stood there, kissing, or how they would have ended it—although she had a nasty feeling that it wouldn't have been her who called a halt. As it turned out, the decision was taken out of their hands, or their lips, or whatever other organs were driving the kiss.

One moment they were deep in the kiss, oblivious to anything but the heat surging between them. The next a gust of wind blew up the hill, turned the umbrella inside out and hurled a sky's worth of rain into their faces. It was like being pitched into a river without warning.

Gasping in shock, Simon and Clara jerked apart. 'Yeurgh…!' Pointlessly, Clara tried to rub the rain from her eyes while Simon cursed as he wrestled the umbrella back into shape.

Eventually he managed to get it the right way out and held it above their heads, but by then they were both drenched and Clara was shivering. 'So much for romance,' he said, his voice the only dry thing about them. 'Still, I think I needed that!'

Take it lightly, Clara told herself. She wrung out her hair and wiped her cheeks with the back of her hand, not that it made much difference. 'Well, it took your mind off your feet, didn't it?'

'It certainly did that.'

'It works better when you're in love,' she added, just in case he misinterpreted the eagerness of her response to him.

'I'll take your word for it,' said Simon. 'Look,

I've had enough rain, if you don't mind. Can we go somewhere dry and unromantic?'

The romance of rain was rather lost on Clara too by that point. Her teeth were chattering, and water from her wet hair was running down her neck. She was more than happy to follow Simon into the first café they came across. It turned out to be a cosy bistro, and they sat together on a banquette near the fire where they could hang up their sodden coats and steam gently in the warmth.

Simon took charge, ordering a bottle of red wine and *steak-frites* in excruciating but effective French, while Clara plucked at her damp clothes and grimaced.

The wine made her feel much better, though, and as she began to dry out she looked around her, because that was easier than looking at Simon and remembering that kiss.

It had ended so suddenly. One minute locked together, the next running for shelter. Clara could almost believe that it had never happened at all.

Except for the fact that her lips were still tingling, and her heart was still thudding and every last cell in her body was sulking at the interruption.

And except for the fact her senses jumped with

awareness when Simon had finished hanging up their coats and sat down beside her.

It was just as well that gust had blown the umbrella inside out when it did, Clara told herself. She had got a bit carried away there, and she didn't want to give Simon the impression that she was unprofessional. She was supposed to be focusing on her career, after all.

And it wasn't as if the kiss had meant anything to either of them. Simon clearly wasn't that bothered. He certainly didn't look as if he was twitching with awareness or wondering how she would react if he laced his fingers with hers and tugged her towards him.

Clara cleared her throat. Not that she was wondering that either.

Not at all.

So, back to business.

She rummaged in her bag for her phone. 'I should ring Ted and find out where they are. I think they'd be interested to see this place.'

'Why?' said Simon, looking around him. 'It's all right, but it's pretty tatty, isn't it?' He fingered a jagged tear in the plastic banquette seat. 'Look at this. And the menus are grubby. As for the wine…' he took a sip from his glass '…a fruity little paint-stripper.'

He broke off as he caught Clara's eye, and flung up a hand. 'Don't tell me! This is romantic too?'

'Well, it *is*. OK, the banquettes have seen better days, but they're so private and so Parisian,' she said. 'I like the fact that there are no white table-cloths or fancy menus. No tourists, either,' she noted, inspecting the few fellow guests. 'It's authentic.'

Simon sighed. 'Is there *any*where that isn't romantic to you?'

'This is exactly the kind of tucked-away place we want you and Stella to have your discussion,' said Clara, searching for Ted's number on her contact list. 'Intimate, private. Waiters in long white aprons, the smell of garlic, *Madame* at the till…it's perfect!'

Ted and the rest of the crew were also in Montmartre, it seemed. They appeared a few minutes later and when they saw what Clara and Simon were eating, ordered lunch too. Even Simon had to admit that the food was excellent, Clara thought. She was very glad that Ted agreed with her about shooting a scene between Simon and Stella over dinner.

By the time she had talked to *Madame*, made all the necessary arrangements and called a couple of taxis to take them back to the hotel, Clara was feeling much more in control. She was back in production assistant mode. Calm, efficient, resourceful…not at all the kind of girl who would kiss the talent or make a fool of herself by wanting to kiss him again.

Really, there was no need to make a fuss about it. It wasn't as if she or Simon would want to repeat it, and no one else would ever guess they had kissed at all.

'What's going on between you and Simon Valentine?' Ted asked under his breath as they made their way out to the taxis.

'What do you mean?' asked Clara, miffed that he had apparently picked up on something. After she had been so careful to behave normally too!

'You're being too polite to him.'

'I'm being *professional*.'

'And he keeps looking at you, whenever you're not looking at him.'

'Really, Ted, I don't know what you're talking about.'

He looked at her closely. Sometimes it was a curse to have a friend who knew you too well.

'You've fallen for the Dow-Jones Darling, too, haven't you?'

'Don't be ridiculous.' Ted would never let her forget it if he knew about the kiss. 'I'm still getting over Matt, remember? I'm here to do my job and nothing else.'

And that meant not kissing Simon again.

By the time they all got back to the hotel, Roland and Stella had arrived and were having a drink in the bar. Stella was instantly recognizable. Clara had never watched her show, but she had seen Stella plenty of times, smiling out from magazine covers at supermarket checkouts everywhere.

'There you are!' Roland beckoned Clara and Simon over, while Ted and the crew took the opportunity to slip away.

Lucky things, thought Clara. Roland was looking displeased, and she guessed that Stella hadn't been happy to discover that Simon wasn't waiting for her. Stella's ratings might have been dropping recently, but there was plenty of the star about her still. Stella was used to having whatever she wanted and, if Ted was to be believed, she wanted Simon.

Eyes narrowed, Clara watched as Stella greeted him effusively and offered perfumed cheeks for a mwah-mwah kiss. She was petite and very pretty, with a gloss of celebrity that made her look faintly unreal. Her hair was just a little too blonde, her teeth too white, her make-up too perfect.

Nothing that anyone could ever accuse Clara of. 'What on earth have you been doing?' Roland demanded, scowling at her. 'You look a bloody mess,' he said bluntly.

Clara looked down at herself. Until that moment, she had forgotten how bedraggled she must look after her drenching. Her boots were still damp, her jacket stained and wrinkled, and she hadn't given a thought to her hair after squeezing out the worst of the rain.

'We were looking for locations,' she said. 'We got a bit wet.'

Roland turned to Simon. 'Please tell me Clara didn't drag you out to look at locations in this rain?'

'She was explaining the romance of Paris in the rain,' Simon said. His eyes met Clara's fleetingly. 'It was very instructive.'

Stella, Clara noticed, had kept a possessive hand on Simon's arm. Now she shuddered lightly. 'We won't be filming in the rain, will we?'

'Of course not,' said Roland quickly.

Simon looked thoughtful. 'You don't think there's something romantic about lovers under an umbrella?' he said, unobtrusively moving away from Stella's clutch.

'Well, now you come to mention it...' Stella fluttered her lashes at him. 'Perhaps it *might* be fun if we did a piece together in the rain.'

It looked as if Ted was right, thought Clara, conscious of a sinking feeling that she chose not to analyse. Stella clearly wasn't planning to play hard to get, although Clara wished her luck in trying to flirt with someone quite as unflirtable as Simon. If Stella wanted Simon to improve her image, she would have to work hard for him.

But perhaps Ted was wrong, and she wasn't interested in Simon's image. Perhaps she was more interested in his mouth and his hands and his lean, solid body.

Something stirred queerly in the pit of Clara's stomach. Only that morning she would have pooh-poohed such an idea, but that was before she had kissed him. Now she could understand it far too easily.

She turned away. 'I'd better go and check the equipment,' she said to Roland.

'I'll go with you,' said Simon quickly. 'I want to change out of these wet things.'

Stella's perfect lips tightened slightly. Clara imagined she was thinking that she was worth a bit of discomfort, but there was only the tiniest of hesitations before she offered a dazzling smile.

'Of course. We'll have a chance to talk properly tonight, anyway. Roland is taking us to the Tour d'Argent.'

'That would have been nice, but I'm afraid I've already agreed to have dinner with Clara here and the rest of the crew,' said Simon pleasantly.

Stella registered Clara's presence for the first time. Her blue gaze took in the hair hanging in rats' tails around Clara's face, the neon-green cast on her wrist and the scruffy wardrobe. She was not impressed, and Clara didn't blame her.

'I'm sure they'll manage without you,' she said to Simon, dimpling charmingly and peeping a glance at him under her lashes that would have had a lesser man crumbling at her feet. 'I think it's so important that we get to know each other before we start filming.'

'That's true,' said Simon. 'Why don't you and Roland join us, in that case? Clara, you can change the booking, can't you? I'm sure the restaurant can squeeze in another two.' He turned back to Stella before Clara could reply. 'You'd love this place, Stella—but perhaps you and Roland would rather go to the Tour d'Argent?'

Clara felt almost sorry for Stella as conflicting emotions crossed the flawless face. Obviously Stella didn't enjoy having her will crossed, but just as obviously she wasn't ready to give up a chance of seducing Simon, and had no intention of being stuck with Roland all night.

'No, it sounds like fun to eat with the crew, don't you think, Roland?' To give her credit, Stella managed a smile, even if it was on the tight side.

Clara avoided Roland's accusing glare. 'I'll give the restaurant a ring,' she said, backing away towards the lift. 'I'll go and do that now.'

Simon was halfway to the lift too. 'You're not to leave me alone with that woman,' he muttered to Clara under his breath.

'I'm sure you're more than a match for Stella.' Clara was ashamed of the lift of her heart.

'That's what you think. Women like that terrify me. They're all breathy voices and fluttery hands, but pure tungsten under the fluff. It's been like this ever since Astrid left,' he grumbled. 'They latch on to you, and before you know it you're taking them out to dinner, and then they invite you in for a coffee and next thing you're expected to ring them every five minutes.'

Shoving his hands in his pockets, he eyed the lift doors morosely.

'Most men would be grateful,' Clara pointed out.

Simon's mention of Astrid had come just in time. Like a fool, she had just allowed herself to believe that he really liked her. Why else would he make it so clear that he preferred her company to Stella's? A little glow had settled around her heart, but it was fading fast at the reminder of Astrid.

How could she have forgotten the woman Simon really wanted?

The way Matt had really wanted Sophie.

'Stella is gorgeous. Men all over the country fantasise about her wanting to spend the evening with them!'

'I don't like being pursued.' The lift doors slid open and they stepped in. 'Why can't women accept a man can be perfectly happy on his own?' he asked grouchily.

'You're not, though. You want Astrid back.'

'Well, I don't want anyone else,' said Simon. 'I certainly don't want to get involved with Stella Holt!'

What was the point of feeling disappointed? Clara asked herself as she checked every connecting cable and tested the batteries in the mikes. What had she expected? That one kiss in the rain would make Simon forget about Astrid and fall in love with her?

It hadn't even been a real kiss. She had just been a distraction from his wet feet.

Besides, she didn't want Simon either. He was *so* not her type, Clara reminded herself. OK, maybe he was more attractive than she had thought at first, and yes, he was a great kisser, but she was only just getting over Matt. There was no way she was putting herself through the agony of falling for a man who really wanted someone else again!

Astrid was perfect for Simon. Cool, clever Astrid. *I don't want anyone else,* he had said. If he was prepared to make just a little effort, Clara was sure he could get Astrid back, and then he would be happy again.

And she would be pleased for him. Really, she would.

Meanwhile, she needed to focus on her career.

She had something to prove to her over-achieving family.

And to herself.

Clara ticked the tripod off her list. Roland had promised her a chance at producing if this programme was a success. She should be thinking about that, and not about the dizzying warmth of Simon's mouth on hers. About how good it would feel to tell her parents that she was a producer now, not about how good it had felt with Simon's arm solid around her.

That kiss had been a mistake. She wouldn't think about it again, Clara vowed. It had been a momentary indulgence, that was all, and it was time to pull herself together. Ted had promised to take her dancing after dinner. That would make her feel better.

She could forget everything when she was dancing.

Even that kiss.

She hoped.

Where was Clara? Backed against the bar, Simon kept a grim eye on the lifts. Turning up at the time agreed had clearly been a mistake. The MediaOchre crew obviously weren't bothered about punctuality, and he had been alone when Stella floated into the bar, looking glamorous and sultry and utterly terrifying.

Now she had him pinned into the bar, and was rabbiting on about how much she loved watching him on the news. She was standing too close, and her perfume was giving him a headache. There was something suffocating about her. She was one of those women who liked to touch you all the time. Simon had to grit his teeth to stop himself brushing her hand away.

He was feeling very twitchy. For all her fluffy femininity, he sensed a steely purpose in Stella. She had set her sights on him—God only knew why!—and intended to have him. Simon didn't care for feeling like a gazelle to her lion. He had *told* Clara not to leave him alone with Stella, but had she listened? No! She was probably still upstairs, singing in the shower she had spent so much time oohing and aahing over.

His mind stumbled at the thought of Clara, wet and naked, and as his eyes focused on Stella's lovely face, he felt oddly winded.

'Don't you agree?' said Stella with a winsome look.

'What?'

Stella's laugh was silvery and notably lacking in humour. 'Simon, I do believe you haven't been listening to a word I said!'

It was true. Simon made an effort to pull himself together. It wasn't like him to be thrown off his stride, but he had been aghast at how clearly he had been able to imagine Clara under the shower, all long legs and soft breasts, her face tilted up to the spray, her hair streaming down her back. Her eyes would be squeezed shut against the water, and she might be holding her cast out of the shower, but she would be singing, he was sure of that.

And she would be swaying from side to side, shimmying her hips, not caring what she looked like.

She wouldn't care if he was watching her. She would just smile that tilting smile of hers and invite him in with her eyes, and she would keep dancing until he slid open the shower door to join her, until he kissed her against the tiles and let his hands roam over her wet, supple body.

Simon's mouth dried. God, what was he *thinking*? This was all the fault of that stupid kiss in the rain. It had been madness, and he should never have provoked her into it, but she had been so close and so warm and that easy way she moved had gone to his head.

It had just been a joke, of course. He knew that, Clara knew that. But then suddenly it hadn't been. Suddenly the light-heartedness had intensified into something deeper, sweeter, more urgent. Something that made his blood pound and his mind reel.

And here she came at last.

Simon's heart jerked alarmingly as he caught sight of Clara crossing the lobby with Ted. She was talking, waving that absurd green cast around, her face animated and her hips swaying. Even if he hadn't been able to see her, he would have known that she was there. Her vibrant presence stirred the air, like an eddy of wind lifting autumn leaves.

Catching sight of him, she smiled and waved, just as if she hadn't left him alone here with Stella.

Simon scowled.

'Aren't you going to be cold?' he asked austerely as she came up.

Clara looked down at herself. On that filthy February night, she had chosen a skirt that swirled and floated around her knees as she walked, a top with thin straps and, in what he supposed was a concession to the weather, a teeny-tiny silky cardigan, all in colours that reminded Simon of nothing so much as a tropical fruit salad. On her feet she wore a pair of bright green shoes with precipitous heels that clashed horribly with the cast on her arm. Next to Stella, in designer black, she looked ridiculous.

Ridiculous, but gorgeous.

'Ted promised we could go dancing after dinner,' said Clara as if that explained everything. 'He's heard of a brilliant salsa club. Do you want to come?'

She included Stella in the question with a friendly smile. Simon could see Stella's lip curling in a sneer. She had already forgone an expensive restaurant in favour of a meal with the crew, and she clearly had no intention of being any more familiar.

'I don't think so, darling,' she said. 'Salsa's not my kind of thing.'

It wasn't Simon's kind of thing either, but he wasn't risking another tête à tête with Stella. 'I'll give it a go.'

'Are you sure, Simon?' Stella's perfectly groomed brows drew together. 'We're shooting tomorrow,' she reminded him. 'You don't want a late night.'

'I'm sure Clara and Ted don't want a late night either. They'll be working too.'

'They're not the ones in front of the camera,' said Stella. 'Tiredness shows up so horribly on film.' She moved a little closer and lowered her voice flirtatiously. 'I was thinking we could come back after dinner and have a quiet session together,' she said. 'We could get to know each other properly and plan what we're going to say.'

'Clara's got that all blocked out, haven't you, Clara?'

Without waiting for Clara's reply, Stella snatched her hand from his arm and flounced off to find Roland. Simon turned to Clara with satisfaction, only to find that she was glaring at him.

'What?'

'Couldn't you be a bit nicer to her?'

Simon was affronted. 'What do you mean?'

'She's not happy. She only agreed to come on the programme because it meant working with you, and if you keep avoiding her she's going to be really miffed,' said Clara worriedly. 'We can't afford to lose her. Stella's got a reputation as a prima donna, and she hates not getting her own way. We don't want her taking her bat and ball and going home because you won't play with her!'

'It's not my fault she can't get the hint that I'm not interested in her,' grumbled Simon.

'It'll be your fault if we can't make the pro-gramme. We really need the two of you, Simon. It's only until tomorrow.' Clara looked at him pleadingly. 'Couldn't you pretend to be interested in her, or at least not give her the brush-off just yet? You know how much the programme means to MediaOchre. It's make or break for us.'

She must have seen the stubbornness in Simon's expression because she held out her cast and winced.

Simon rolled his eyes. 'Isn't that old cast trick getting old?'

'It's jolly sore.' She rapped the knuckles of her good hand on the cast. 'Ouch.'

Simon sighed.

'You know, I didn't think you were the kind of man who would stand by and let the woman who saved your mother's bag suffer the agony of uncertainty,' Clara went on, shaking her head in disappointment. 'I do believe the word "heroine" was bandied around,' she remembered artlessly, 'but that obviously doesn't mean anything to you. If it did, you'd never let me face the collapse of the company and the loss of my job, just because you couldn't be bothered to be nice to your co-presenter.

'But I can see that's too much to ask,' she went on, clearly enjoying herself. 'I suppose I'll just have to find another job. Oh, and somewhere else to live, because I certainly won't be able to pay the rent any more. I won't be able to go and stay with Ted, because he'll lose his flat too, so we'll be wandering the streets together. But we'll be fine,' she said bravely. 'Don't worry about us.'

'Oh, very well,' said Simon, goaded. 'I'll be nice to Stella.'

'Promise?'

'Promise. But I'm not sleeping with her,' he warned. 'My mother's bag wasn't worth that much!'

So he had to sit next to Stella at dinner, and let her monopolise his attention, while Clara, all smiles, had a great time at the other end of the table with the cameraman, Steve, and Peter, the sound guy.

Restored to good humour by his attention, Stella was fluttering her lashes at him over the rim of

her glass. 'My accountant says I should be invest-
ing my money, but what do you think? I'm just
so confused by finance.'

Suppressing a sigh, Simon set his jaw and explained how the markets operated while at the
other end of the table Clara threw back her head
and laughed at some joke Steve had told, and Ted
and Roland were immersed in a long discussion
which Simon strongly suspected was intended to
leave him at the mercy of Stella.

Evidently taking his gritty conversation as encouragement, Stella inched her chair closer. She
found excuses to touch his thigh, his arm, his
knee, and only the memory of Clara's smile at
his promise stopped Simon from edging back
into Roland's lap. Stella was monumentally self-
absorbed, he decided. She ignored everyone
except Roland, snapped at waiters, and pushed
her food away barely touched.

When at last the meal was over, Stella started
dropping hints that the two of them should head
back to the hotel alone, but Simon felt he had
endured enough by then.

'I said I'd go dancing,' he said, trying to sound
regretful.

Stella flicked a dismissive glance down the

table to where Clara was telling some uproari-
ous story. 'They'll just be going to some ghastly
club and getting drunk,' she said. 'You know what
crews are like. They're halfway there already, I'd
say,' she added contemptuously.

'Someone ought to tell that girl Clara that she
can't carry off those colours,' she went on, when
Simon didn't respond. 'Still, I suppose she has
to get attention some way. She's not exactly a
stunner, is she?' Complacent in her own beauty,
Stella smoothed her fingers along her clavicle.
'It's a shame she ends up looking so vulgar.'

'I think she's attractive,' said Simon stiffly, and
Stella's celestial blue eyes sharpened.

'Be careful, darling. You're quite an innocent
in the world of television, I can tell. These production companies are full of girls like Clara
who just sleep their way to the top. I've seen her
eyeing you up.'

'That's ridiculous. I've got no influence in television.'

'You'd be surprised,' said Stella. 'I'm quite sure
Clara knows just how useful you could be to her.
Anyway, she's having a good time with the crew.
They won't mind if you and I go back to the hotel

and get cosy with a little *digestif*. Wouldn't you rather do that than go to some noisy club?'

Simon wasn't over-enamoured of the club idea, but he would rather cosy up to a crocodile with PMT than be alone with Stella. Mindful of Clara's instructions, though, he bit back the comment and forced an approximation of a smile. 'I won't be long.'

Stella put her lips close to his ear. 'Knock on my door when you get back.'

It was a huge relief when she made Roland take her back to the hotel. As soon as they had gone, the rest of the party relaxed and headed off for the club. 'Thank you. ' Clara smiled at Simon. 'Stella looked much happier when she left.'

'I don't want to hear any more about being nice to her,' said Simon. 'She got a free financial consultation out of me!'

'And I appreciate it,' Clara promised him. 'Now you can relax and enjoy yourself.'

They were pushing their way into a crowded bar, and they had to raise their voices over the sound of the catchy salsa beat. Clara's feet were tapping. 'Come on, let's dance,' she said, grabbing his hand unselfconsciously, but Simon dug in his heels at that.

'I don't dance.'

Clara stopped and stared at him. 'Why on earth did you come then?'

'It was a choice between this and a nightcap with Stella, and I've been nice enough to her tonight.'

'Well, since you're here, you ought to try it. Dancing's good for you.'

Simon grunted. 'I fail to see how making a fool of myself on the dance floor could possibly be good for me.'

'It's about letting go.'

Exactly the reason he didn't dance.

'I don't do letting go either,' said Simon.

'Well, *I'm* dancing.'

Clara disappeared into the crowd, and Simon found a spot to lean against the wall with a lager. It was dark and very hot, and the smell of beer and sweat fought with the throb of music in the darkness. Every surface was sticky as far as Simon could make out. He could feel the clagginess of the floor every time he moved his feet.

Astrid liked the theatre, or classical music. Simon had gone with her occasionally but usually they went to receptions, to drinks parties or expensive restaurants where it was all very quiet and tasteful, and there were no grinding, gyrating bodies, no pounding music reverberating up through the floor.

Simon felt as if he had been transported to a different world. Once his eyes had adjusted to the dim light, he kept getting glimpses of Clara through the crush on the dance floor. She was impossible to miss with that neon-green cast.

Not that it seemed to be cramping her style. Her skirt swirled up round her thighs and her arms waved and her body swayed and spun. Simon couldn't take his eyes off her. She was like a flame, dancing and flickering mesmerizingly in the darkness.

Sometimes she danced with Ted, sometimes on her own, but sometimes with other men, strangers presumably. Simon watched, scowling, as they put their hands on Clara's waist, or swung her round them, their hips thrusting suggestively. Why didn't they just get a room? Simon wondered savagely.

God, there was another one! His fingers tightened around his glass. Dressed like a gigolo in a vest and obscenely tight jeans, he was undulating around Clara, and she was *laughing*! Dammit, couldn't she see the guy was a slime ball, and

probably a pervert to boot? She shouldn't be allowed out on her own.

The music was just coming to an end, thank
God, but Simon saw the slime ball shout something in Clara's ear, obviously suggesting another
dance.

Simon couldn't bear it any longer. Smacking
down the glass he had been nursing on a nearby
table, he stalked onto the floor.

CHAPTER SIX

'My turn, I think,' Simon said, taking her by the arm and giving her admirer such a glare that the man threw up his hands, shrugged and retreated.

'I thought you didn't dance?' said Clara, but the music had started again and she had to lean close and shout in his ear.

'I don't,' he shouted back. 'I can hold you, though. Will that do?'

Without giving her a chance to reply, he put one hand at the small of her back and drew her close, holding her good hand against his chest with his other. Clara stared at him for a moment, then rested the hand with its absurd cast on his shoulder and relaxed into him.

Simon could feel the warmth of her body through her flimsy top. She was soft and supple, and she swayed in an attempt to dance while he shuffled around a bit, which was the best he could do. *He* wasn't going to gyrate in tight trousers and a vest.

Luckily, the music had slowed, but it was still

impossible to talk, and Simon was glad of it. Succumbing to temptation, he rested his cheek against her hair. It felt silky against his skin, and he breathed in the same fresh scent he had noticed earlier that day. There on the crowded floor, with the other dancers jostling around them and the music making the floor vibrate, for the first time in as long as he could remember, Simon felt himself relax.

Which was odd because there was nothing restful about Clara. She was all warmth and movement and challenge, and he liked coolness and calmness and control. That was what had always attracted him to Astrid.

Simon frowned slightly against Clara's hair. It worried him that he had been in Paris less than twenty-four hours and already he was having trouble picturing Astrid clearly. All he remembered was an impression of serenity and contentment. It was always easy to be with Astrid. She never made him walk in the rain or dance in dark, noisy clubs.

So he should be thinking about getting Astrid back, not about how warm and soft Clara was. It was Astrid he really wanted.

Wasn't it?

* * *

Clara shut the hotel room door and leant back against it, letting out a long breath as she closed her eyes. Her heart was still thudding from that last dance with Simon.

By unspoken agreement, they had left when it had ended. Ted, Steve and Peter were ready to move on to another bar, but Clara and Simon had come back to the hotel. There had been silence in the taxi but Clara's body was thrumming with awareness, and her pulse was roaring in her ears so loudly that she was sure Simon must be able to hear it.

He must know that her senses were still jerking, that her back felt as if the imprint of his palm were seared onto it, that her fingers tingled where he had held her. It had been so, so tempting to lean closer, to let her hand slide a little higher up onto his shoulder. She tried not to, but how could she help remembering how easily they had kissed before? If they had turned their faces just a little way, they could have kissed again, but Simon kept his cheek against her hair, and she kept staring at his collar.

Which was just as well.

Because what a mistake that would have been. Simon didn't need another groupie, fantasising about that lean, angular body and that cool, cool mouth. Clara couldn't understand how she had missed the appeal of it before. Now she couldn't think about anything else.

But that was pointless. For a start, it was deeply unprofessional to lust after the talent, quite apart from the fact that she would be treading on Stella's toes and possibly putting the whole programme at risk.

Hadn't she vowed to focus on her career? It wasn't long since she had been desperate about Matt, Clara reminded herself. She had had enough of longing for someone who was hopelessly out of reach. She was tired of being liked, but not quite enough to be more than second best.

Simon had been very clear. He needed Astrid, just as Matt had needed Sophie. *I don't want anyone else,* Simon had said.

He might have held her close on the dance floor, but he didn't want any more than that. Why else would he have simply wished her a cool good-night in the lift?

Deliberately, Clara made herself remember those terrible weeks after Matt had left. The jagged pain in her heart, the aching loneliness. The bitter realisation that all she could do was put one foot in front of another and trudge on without him.

She had survived. More than survived. Brick by brick, joke by joke, she had built up a defensive barrier of gaiety around her heart and it had served her well. She wasn't going to let it crumble now, not for a man who was clearly interested in another woman, no matter how good it felt when he held her.

No matter how well he kissed.

Sighing, Clara pushed herself away from the door. She was very tired, almost too tired to enjoy this lovely room. The bed was wide, inviting, with crisp white linen. It was a shame not to have someone to share it with, and her mind flickered treacherously to Simon, who was making do in the basic room that had been hers, Simon, on whom the romance of this room would have been quite wasted.

Clara stepped out onto the balcony. It had stopped raining while they were in the club, but the roads were still wet. She could hear tyres swishing on the tarmac, and the occasional horn. Laughter and music spilled out of a bar down the street, and the air shimmered with the pulse of the city.

Hugging her arms together, Clara looked down onto the courtyard, where the cobbles gleamed in the yellow light that spilled out of the lobby windows. It was perfect, just like the room behind her was perfect, and she sighed again, depressed and lonely and aware that, for the first time in years, it wasn't Matt she most wished for.

But there was no point in wishing for Simon. He wouldn't appreciate this anyway. He had no idea about romance. Matt would have done, if he'd been here, but Simon would tell her she would catch her death, and for God's sake come in and close the window.

He wouldn't draw her down onto those white sheets and make love to her all night. He would remind her that they had to get up early next morning and make sure that she had set the alarm.

Clara crawled into the bed. She was exhausted, but she couldn't sleep. She lay luxuriating in the soft sheets and trying not to feel lonely. Trying not to think about that kiss or how it had felt dancing with Simon—if you could call it dancing! The man had no sense of rhythm.

It had been like trying to dance with a block of wood, Clara thought, encouraging the train of thought. So what if he had strong hands and a solid body and a mouth that made the air leak out of her lungs? She could never fall for a man who couldn't dance.

Never.

She had just drifted off to sleep when there was a tap at the door. She rolled over with a groan and pulled the pillow over her head, but the tap came again. If Ted had lost his room key again, she was officially going to demote him from best friend to most annoying colleague imaginable.

Blearily, Clara rolled out of bed and grabbed the throw to cover her nakedness. Ted was a good friend, but not that good. She was still wrapping it round her when she opened the door in mid yawn.

'This had better—'

She broke off. Stella stood there, dressed in a sheer negligee that left little to the imagination, her hand raised to knock once more.

There was a moment of appalled silence as they stared at each other.

'I see,' said Stella, blue eyes blazing. 'So that's how it is! I warned Simon about you, but did he listen?'

'What? No!' Clara came abruptly awake. 'Wait!'

she said, realising too late what Stella had assumed. 'Wait, Simon's not here!'

But Stella was already stalking back to her room next door and, by the time Clara had tripped over the cover and disentangled herself, the door had slammed.

That was the end of Clara's sleep that night.

Stella woke Roland and screamed at him down the phone. Roland rang Clara and screamed at her.

'What the hell are you doing sleeping with Simon Valentine?'

In vain did Clara try and explain that she and Simon had just swapped rooms. At two in the morning Stella insisted on being found another equally luxurious hotel. 'I'm not staying here to be humiliated another moment, and if you think I'm taking part in your pathetic programme, you can forget it!'

Ted, on his way back to bed, returned to the hotel in time to see Stella flouncing out, and the realisation that his programme had just lost one of its stars.

'I'm going to call Simon,' he said, when he'd heard the story from a desperate Clara. 'Perhaps he can talk some sense into Stella.'

Only Simon could be woken at two in the morning and look as crisp and capable as ever. Clara had an absurd desire to burst into tears when he walked into Roland's room, where they had gathered.

Still buttoning his cuffs, his gaze swept around the room. Incandescent with fury, Roland was pacing in a magnificent dressing gown, while Ted hunched on a chair, his head in his hands. Clara was still wrapped in the coverlet, and her expression must have been desperate for Simon's brows snapped together.

'What in God's name is going on?'

In the end, it was Ted who explained the situation, with unhelpful interruptions from Roland, who blamed Clara for everything.

'What were you thinking, changing rooms, anyway?' he bellowed. 'Simon was supposed to be in that room! Of course Stella was going to think you were sleeping with him!'

'It was my idea,' said Simon levelly. 'It's not Clara's fault. And it's not as if it's the end of the world, anyway.'

With an effort, Roland clamped down on the obvious retort, which was that it was Simon's fault for not letting himself be seduced by Stella.

'Easy for you to say! You haven't spent half your budget on a programme that's not going to happen!'

'You can make the programme without Stella, can't you?'

'Not really,' said Ted. 'We sold it on the basis of the two of you.' He hesitated. 'I don't suppose you'd consider going after Stella, maybe tomorrow when she's calmed down a bit?' he asked hopefully.

'You suppose right,' said Simon. 'If you ask me, you're better off without her. It's unprofessional to have a tantrum over something so silly. I didn't think she had anything of interest to say in any case.'

'The whole point of the programme was the contrast between two points of view,' Roland said tightly. 'It's not going to work with one presenter, and we can't afford to get anyone else out here, even if we could arrange it at short notice.'

The three of them started worrying away at the problem, putting forward increasingly wild suggestions that the other two would shoot down as impractical.

Simon listened in increasing exasperation. The solution seemed obvious to him.

'Why can't Clara do it?'

They all stopped and stared at him. 'What?'

'Clara could take Stella's place.'

'Clara?' echoed Roland with unflattering incredulity. 'Are you mad?' He had evidently forgotten that he was talking to his only remaining presenter. 'Clara couldn't do it!'

'Why not?'

'For a start, she doesn't have any experience.'

Simon turned to Clara. 'You told me you'd done some acting.'

'Well, yes, a little, but—'

'We're not looking for a song and dance routine,' Roland interrupted. 'What we need is glamour and, not to put too fine a point on it, Clara doesn't have the looks.'

'At least she's here, and hasn't stormed off in a huff,' said Simon, who was feeling guilty, and then cross with himself for feeling that way. No one had told him he was expected to take Stella to bed to keep her sweet! He'd done his best at dinner, hadn't he?

But Clara looked so devastated, and he remembered how important this wretched programme was to her. It wasn't her fault that Stella couldn't take a hint.

'You know, it might work,' said Ted.

'How?' Roland was too angry to be tactful. 'Look at her! Does she look like a presenter to you?'

Clara shifted under the gaze of the three men, and tucked the coverlet more tightly round her. 'I dare say she can put some decent clothes on,' said Simon, distracted by the creaminess of her bare shoulders.

'Oh, I don't know.' Clara lifted her chin and made a brave attempt at a recovery. 'Coverlets are bang on trend this year.'

Roland ignored that. 'And what about that stupid cast on her arm?'

'We could shoot round her,' said Ted eagerly. 'It'll be much easier for Simon if he's got some-one to talk to on camera. Clara can put the pro-romance point of view so they're having a conversation. We've got two cameras, so we can shoot both of them, but we can always edit Clara out if necessary later.'

'Great,' said Clara. 'I've always wanted to be edited out!'

But Roland seemed to be considering the matter at least. He rubbed his nose. 'But what am I going to say to Channel 16? They're expecting Stella, or someone with a similar profile at least.'

'Tough,' said Simon in a flat voice. 'It's Clara or no one if you want me involved. You can have me, or you can grovel to Stella, in which case I'll be the one flouncing off. I'm not working with that woman again!'

'This is the best option, Roland,' said Ted.

'Don't you think you'd better ask Clara if she's prepared to do it?' Simon interrupted.

'Of course I'll do it,' said Clara as they turned to look expectantly at her. 'I'll do whatever it takes to save the programme. You can cut me out later.'

'You're looking tense.'

'Of course I'm tense,' snapped Clara. 'I've put the entire programme in jeopardy! I'll be lucky if Roland lets me keep my job, and if I make a mess of today, I'll be lucky if there's a job to keep.'

On top of which, her eyes felt as if they were bulging with lack of sleep, her wrist was aching, and Roland's remarks about her unimpressive appearance had stung more than Clara wanted to admit. She had done her best to brush up that morning but, short of a fairy godmother to wave a wand, there wasn't that much she could do to transform herself into a glamorous Stella looka-like.

All in all, her confidence was down in her un-glamorous boots. Now she was expected to spar-kle in front of the camera—and Simon wondered why she was tense!

They were standing in one of the semi-circular embrasures on the Pont Neuf, looking down onto the Seine, while Peter manoeuvred a boom over their heads and Ted and Steve discussed camera angles. Having thrown off the rain overnight, Paris had confounded them with a beautiful day. It was still cold, but the sky was a bright, brilliant blue and the city seemed to be preening itself in the winter sunshine.

Clara was in no mood to appreciate it, though. Roland never got involved in the practicalities of filming and, anyway, he was still too angry to speak to her. Even if MediaOchre Productions survived this debacle, he would sack her as soon as they got back to London, Clara was miserably sure.

'He can hardly sack you because I didn't want to sleep with Stella,' said Simon when she told him that, but Clara wouldn't be comforted.

'I shouldn't have upset her by being in your room.' She hugged her arms together fretfully. 'I just feel so guilty about spoiling everything...'

'Don't you think you're overreacting?' said Simon, crisp as ever. 'I don't see why you're beating yourself up. None of this is your fault.'

But Clara wasn't convinced. 'The whole future of MediaOchre hangs on this programme, and it's not going to work without Stella. You heard what Roland said. I'm too ordinary to be in front of the camera.'

'That's ridiculous,' said Simon shortly. 'I've never met anyone *less* ordinary.'

He studied her. She was wearing jeans today. Since there was no way she was going to rival Stella's sophisticated look, Ted had decided as director that Clara should look casual, but not scruffy. Her red jumper made her look too bulky, he said, so she only had a long-sleeved T-shirt on under her jacket. Ted wouldn't let her have her scarf either.

'What does it matter what I wear?' she had grumbled. 'I thought you were going to edit me out.'

'We'll see,' was all Ted would commit himself to. 'We can't do much about the cast, but it would be good to get in some shots of you as well so Simon doesn't look as if he's talking to himself the whole time.'

So Clara was shivering on the bridge. The sun might be shining, but it was still February. 'I'm freezing,' she said.

'Here.' Simon took off his jacket. 'Put this on until the cameras are rolling.'

'But now you'll be cold,' Clara objected, even as she hugged his jacket gratefully around her shoulders.

'I don't feel the cold.'

The heaviness of the jacket felt very intimate somehow. 'Like you don't dance, and you don't let go?'

Simon glanced at her, and then away. 'Yes, like that.'

There was a tiny silence. Peter was shouting something to Ted about the boom, and a party of tourists eyed them curiously, momentarily distracted from their admiration of Paris's oldest bridge, but for a moment it felt to Clara as if she and Simon were quite alone.

'Look, there's no point in fretting about Stella,' said Simon, watching a pleasure boat slide beneath them, the guide's commentary echoing out over the water. 'You can't do anything about it now. You just have to deal with the situation as it is, and there's no reason why you shouldn't do just as good a job as Stella would have done.'

Clara hunched her shoulders. 'I hate it when people are reasonable.'

'That's a very unreasonable thing to say,' he said, but she thought she saw a smile hovering around his mouth.

'Well, there you are, all ready to enjoy a good old moan, and then someone like you comes along and spoils it by pointing out that things aren't that bad...' Clara sniffed, and that suspicion of a smile became almost a certainty.

'They're not. You'll do fine as a presenter.'

'If I don't freeze to death first—and don't tell me I'm highly unlikely to freeze in the middle of a city in this temperature!'

'You were very eloquent about romance yesterday. Now you just have to do that again, but on camera. Just pretend you're under that umbrella and it's pouring with rain.'

Clara wished he hadn't mentioned the umbrella. Suddenly the memory of the kiss they had shared was throbbing right there between them on the Pont Neuf. Simon could feel it too, she knew he could. Their gazes glanced, jarred, skidded away from each other, and the silence tightened. Her heart was banging against her ribs as she tried to think of a way to break it but, in the end, it was Simon who spoke first.

'Anyway,' he said. Was it her imagination, or did he sound huskier than usual? He stopped and cleared his throat. 'You told me you wanted to be a star,' he reminded her. 'Now's your chance.'

'Getting ready to be edited out of a documentary wasn't quite what I had in mind,' said Clara, gloomy again. She leant back against the old stones, almost able to convince herself now that the sticky moment when the kiss had shimmered between them hadn't really happened. 'I was thinking more a spangled costume and lots of singing and dancing.'

'If you can even *think* of dancing in a spangled costume, you can do this,' said Simon. 'Come on, there must be some inspiring song in your repertoire of musicals!'

'I suppose so.' Clara liked the idea. She mulled over it for a while. 'I could be like Julie Andrews. Remember when she set off to be a governess in *The Sound of Music*?'

'You have to remember that I don't have your

encyclopaedic knowledge of musicals,' he said with asperity.

She straightened, clutching the jacket around her, her face vivid with new enthusiasm. 'You must remember! She was nervous about taking on a Captain and seven children.'

'I imagine she would be.'

'And she sings herself into feeling confident.'

Simon was just congratulating himself on having restored the brightness to her face when she launched into the song—some nonsense about having confidence in sunshine and rain—and, being Clara, she didn't hum it under her breath the way anyone else would have done. No, she belted it out as if the Pont Neuf were her stage, and the passers-by her audience. One or two smiled, but most averted their eyes and hurried past.

Simon was tempted to do the same. '*Clara*...I didn't want a demonstration. I just wanted you to feel more confident.'

'It worked!' said Clara, arms outstretched, feet tapping.

He pinched the bridge of his nose. 'Ted, can we get on before she makes even more of an exhibition of herself?'

But Ted already had the camera pointing their way. 'Sure,' he said. 'Shut up, Clara. Let's start.'

Clara gave Simon back his jacket. 'Did you know that the Pont Neuf is one of the top ten places to make a marriage proposal? It's what makes Paris one of the most romantic cities in the world.'

'A romantic city is just a myth manufactured by marketing teams,' Simon said. 'It's got nothing to do with relationships, and everything to do with what tourism contributes to the economy. In the case of Paris, that's a lot.'

And they were off, arguing backwards and forwards about whether or not romance was real or not. Clara was so absorbed in their discussion that she forgot about Peter dangling the mike from an eight-foot pole over their heads. She forgot about the cameras, and her nervousness and even the whole fiasco with Stella. There was just Simon, stubbornly refusing to accept that love could change everything, and that there was magic in the most ordinary things if you cared to look for it.

From the Pont Neuf, they wandered around the Ile de la Cité. They paused to admire Notre Dame, climbed the Eiffel Tower, and strolled down the Champs-Élysées. Clara was still acting as production assistant, so ran backwards and forwards, checking permissions and equipment and making notes for Ted, then rushing back to Simon, waiting imperturbably in front of the camera, and picking up the argument where they had left off. Every now and then, Ted would make them back up and start the discussion again, and Clara soon lost track of whether the cameras were filming them or not.

They broke at lunch, and Clara was glad to go back to the hotel and crash for a few hours. She felt better after a nap and a shower and, by the time they were back at the restaurant in Montmartre, she was much more herself again.

Simon had raised his brows when she turned up in exactly the same outfit as the night before, but as she pointed out, she didn't have an extensive wardrobe to choose from. 'I wasn't expecting to be in front of the camera,' she told him. 'This is as smart as I can get.'

Madame welcomed them back to the restaurant and had kept them a secluded table as arranged. Clara handed out clearance forms to all the other diners, making sure they wouldn't object if their image was glimpsed on screen, and with Ted ordered a meal that would be easy to eat on camera.

'No spaghetti,' she told Simon as she slid into

the banquette opposite him. 'We vetoed snails, mussels and crayfish as well. Too messy.'

'I'm glad to see Ted's allowed us some wine,' he said, pouring her a glass from the bottle that had arrived compliments of the house. 'Are we allowed to start?'

'I think so. They'll be ages yet.'

Simon glanced across the restaurant to where Ted and Steve had their heads together. 'What are they doing?'

'They're setting up a two shot. It's better with two cameras. If they get them in the right place, they can film us both at the same time from a distance instead of swinging the camera from face to face, or having to do those awful noddy shots, where you ask the questions again and nod encouragingly when the interview is over.'

'They do that sometimes after I've done a piece for the news.'

'Of course. I forget that you know all about television.'

'I've got to admit that this is more interesting,' said Simon. 'I'm usually just sitting in my office—and there's never any wine included!'

Clara eyed him over the rim of her glass. 'So you're not regretting I persuaded you into taking part?'

'I think I'd use the word blackmail rather than persuasion,' he said, and she laughed.

'It hasn't been that bad, has it?'

'What, apart from being made to stand around in the pouring rain, dodging the seduction attempts of a monstrously self-absorbed chat show hostess, being woken at two in the morning and standing around half the day waiting for Ted to decide on the light he wants?'

'See, I knew you'd have a good time!'

Simon took a sip of his wine. The truth was that he *had* been enjoying himself, much to his own surprise.

'It makes a change from my usual routine,' was all he would concede, though.

'So what would you be doing if you were at home now?' asked Clara, settling back into the banquette.

He glanced at the clock on the wall. It was nearly half past eight. 'Working, probably.'

'It doesn't sound to me like you have enough fun.'

'Fun is overrated,' said Simon flatly.

Clara was dismayed. 'That's sad.'

'No, what's sad is when people throw away perfectly good lives just for momentary fun.' He couldn't keep the bitterness from his voice. 'My father was a great believer in fun. He liked to do things on the spur of the moment, the more extravagant and exciting the better. He'd come and take me out of school without warning, and we'd go hang-gliding or sailing, or we'd be on a plane for a weekend's skiing. "Let's have some fun", he'd say.'

'It sounds like a great childhood,' said Clara with a touch of envy. 'My parents were the opposite. I mean, they weren't cruel or anything, but their minds were always on their research. I spent my childhood either being dragged round medieval churches or being told to be quiet so they could read. I was forever being banished to the bottom of the garden to practice my song and dance routines because I was giving them a headache.'

She tried to imagine her own father, vague about anything that didn't relate to ecclesiastical architecture, whisking her out of school to go skiing for the weekend.

'My family's idea of fun is to discover a medieval pyx they haven't seen before, and they can get really animated about double hammer-beam roofs or wardmote court records,' she said, reassured to see that Simon was looking baffled. 'They spent all of last Christmas dinner arguing about later Franciscan thought instead of discussing the TV Christmas specials like a normal family.'

She sighed. 'I wouldn't have minded a bit of fun.'

'At least your parents take their work seriously,' said Simon. 'My father never took anything seriously. He inherited his money, and never thought about where it came from. In theory, he was on the board of a few companies, but it was just an excuse for some good lunches and it never interfered with the real business of life, which was amusing himself.

'I sometimes wonder,' he said, contemplating his wine, 'whether things would have been different if my father had been forced to work for what he wanted, but it was always easy come, easy go with him.'

'You must have some good memories of him, though, don't you?' said Clara. 'It must have been exciting to be taken out of school, wasn't it? And at least he was thinking of you and wanted to be with you.'

Simon's face closed. 'He wasn't thinking of us

when he drove too fast down that mountain road. He wasn't thinking of us when he gambled away most of his inheritance and invested what was left in a scam that a two-year-old should have been able to see through. He was having fun, not thinking about what it would be like for my mother to be left on her own.'

Or what it would be like for his son to lose his father, Clara thought.

'She lost everything,' Simon said. 'Her husband, her house, her car, her money and a lot of her so-called friends. But she did have one good friend, who gave her a job in her dress shop. It was the first job she'd ever had, and she hated it, but she stuck at it until I could earn enough to support us both. Whenever she's at her most exasperating, I remember that.'

Frances had struck Clara as utterly charming, but flighty and frivolous. It was hard to imagine her gritting her teeth and knuckling down to an unfamiliar job. Now Clara could understand why Simon gritted *his* teeth and put up with his mother's extravagances.

'How old were you when your father died?' she asked him.

'Nearly fifteen.'

It must have been hard for him, too, thought Clara, rolling her glass slowly between her hands. It was bad enough losing a father without losing everything else you'd always taken for granted at the same time.

'What happened to you?'

'Well, there was no question of school fees any more, so I switched to the local school.'

'What was that like?' A private schoolboy pitched without warning into the local comprehensive. Clara couldn't imagine that had been easy for him, but he brushed her concern aside.

'It was fine,' he said briefly. Too briefly, Clara couldn't help thinking. 'As soon as I could, I got a part-time job so that I could help my mother and put myself through university. Once I started earning, I made sure that I was never going to be in the position of not having any security again. And I never will be.'

CHAPTER SEVEN

CLARA picked at the dribble of wax that had trickled down the side of the candle, thinking about Simon and how his father's death had turned him from the mischievous little boy Frances Valentine remembered into the self-contained man sitting across the table from her.

Easy now to understand why control was so important to him. No wonder he was so resistant to letting go, to rocking the boat the way Astrid had done and plunging into the tempestuous waters of passion.

'Your mother seemed like a person who still has plenty of fun,' she said cautiously.

'Oh, yes, she's big on fun too,' said Simon with a sigh. 'She'd just got back on her feet and had some security when she threw it all up for someone she met at a party.'

'Gosh, really?'

'She said she was "madly in love".' He hooked his fingers in the air to emphasis the strangeness of the concept. Clara had the sense that the phrase might as well have been in Hungarian for all it meant to him.

'She and Tim had only been together a month when she announced that they were going to get married and live happily ever after,' Simon went on with remembered weariness. 'I suggested that she wait a few months until she knew Tim a bit better but no! I didn't understand, it was *love*.'

He made a face as if the word tasted bad in his mouth. 'Well, it might have been, but it certainly didn't last. They were divorced barely a year after they married, and I had to pick up the pieces again.

'My mother,' he said with evident restraint, 'is not a moderate person. When she's having fun, she's having more fun than anyone else, but when she's down, there's a very, very big mess!'

He sipped his wine, remembering. 'A couple of years later, it was Rob. At least she didn't go as far as getting married that time, but the effect was just as devastating. After Rob, there was Geoffrey, and that ended in tears too...'

Setting down his glass, Simon looked at Clara across the table. 'I don't understand why she keeps putting herself through it,' he said, baffled. 'Is it really worth it?'

'If you'd ever been in love, you'd know that it is,' said Clara. 'Loving means making yourself vulnerable to being hurt, and yes, it is a risk, but if you try and protect yourself against that, you'll never know the wonder of falling in love.'

She twisted the stem of her glass between her fingers, looking at the wine and remembering Matt. Bitter as the ending had been, she wouldn't have missed loving him for anything. 'When you love someone, it just feels so…exhilarating. The whole world seems better, brighter. It's like you feel *connected* in a way you can never be if you're not prepared to open your heart to loving.'

'Is that from a musical?' Simon raised derisive brows, and she flushed a little.

'You can mock, but the reason so many songs from musicals are popular is because they're *true*. People recognize them from their own experience.'

'You can't live your life by a philosophy according to musicals, Clara,' he said astringently.

Ruffled, Clara stuck her chin in the air. 'There are worse philosophies to live by.'

'Dear God.' He shook his head.

'Look, all I'm saying is that you have to be brave to love. It's not just a passive thing that happens to you. You can stay safe and never be hurt, but if you do, you'll never be truly happy either. Your mother knows that. That's why she's prepared to have a go. I admire her for it.'

'Yes, well, you're not the one who has to pick her up when it all goes wrong,' said Simon with a touch of defensiveness. 'It's not even as if your approach has brought you much of this famous happiness. You're still pining for your ex.'

Good point. Clara took a slug of her wine, unwilling to concede. 'I'm not *pining* for him.'

Much.

'When you love someone, you want them to be happy, even if it isn't what you want. I've accepted that Matt is happier with Sophie. Yes, I was unhappy for a time, but I don't regret loving him. Being with Matt was one of the best experiences of my life. I know what it's like to love someone utterly, and how good that feels. If I haven't met anyone else, it's because I won't settle for anything less than that feeling again. That's not pining.'

Simon was unconvinced. 'Maybe not, but it is unrealistic. You're pinning your hopes for the future on some vague, indefinable feeling. You might as well read the stars or consult tea leaves for all the good a "feeling" is going to do you when it comes to thinking about your long-term happiness.

'Isn't it better to get to know someone first?' he went on, leaning over to top up her wine. 'To make sure that you share the same interests, and that you're able to build a relationship on a sound economic footing? Those things are much more likely to give you long-lasting happiness with someone than what is no more than a fleeting sexual attraction.'

Clara's mouth was set in a mulish line. 'Love is about more than sex.'

'Do you really believe that?' he asked sceptically.

'Of course I do! Love is about needing someone, about feeling as if the day isn't quite right if they're not there.' The way she had felt about Matt. 'It's about knowing that, no matter how bad a day you've had, the moment you see them again or hear their voice, the world is back in its place.'

'Uh-oh.' He made a show of looking frantically

around for an escape route. 'I can feel a song coming on!'

Clara ignored him. 'It's about looking at the one you love and feeling your heart swelling and swelling as if it would burst,' she said, pressing her fist against her chest, remembering the power and pain of it. 'It's about feeling a bigger and better and braver person for loving them, about feeling as if you've come home when you can rest against them...'

Feeling the way she never would again.

To her horror, Clara heard her voice crack at the memory, and she took another gulp of wine.

'And you want someone to feel all this for you?' Simon didn't even bother to hide his derision. 'Isn't that a bit of a tall order?'

'Maybe, but it's how I felt about Matt.' The wine had steadied her, thank goodness, and she sounded normal again. 'I know that it's possible. Matt was everything I've ever wanted. He's funny and charming and kind and when I was with him I was in heaven. I want to feel like that again, and I want someone to feel that way about me.

'Go ahead,' she said, her eyes meeting Simon's, 'sneer all you want, but one of these days you'll fall in love, and then you'll know what I mean!'

'That's not going to happen,' said Simon, matter-of-fact as ever. 'Always supposing I believed such a thing were possible, if I were going to fall in love, it would have been with Astrid. We were equals—socially, economically, intellectually—and that's a far better foundation for a lasting relationship than any amount of swelling hearts.'

Well, that was her put in her place, thought Clara. There was no way *she* was ever going to be Simon's economic or intellectual equal.

Not that she cared, she reassured herself hastily. She couldn't imagine anything worse than being stuck with someone who didn't believe in love and insisted on being rational about everything. It would be like being with her family, and always feeling as if she belonged in a parallel universe.

Only it hadn't felt like that when they had kissed.

When Simon kissed her it had felt alarmingly like coming home.

Clara wriggled her shoulders to shake off *that* idea. True, Simon grew more attractive every time she looked at him, but there was no way she was going to fall in love with him. No, no, no. That would never do.

It was just a passing sexual attraction, the way

Simon thought all relationships were. It was important, but it wasn't enough on its own. It wasn't *love*.

'Being equals wasn't enough for Astrid, though, was it?' she said a little pettishly. 'Maybe she wants passion now. Maybe she wants to feel loved and desired. Paolo will make her feel that.'

Simon snorted at the mention of Paolo. 'Astrid will soon get tired of him. What has she got in common with him? Nothing! We've talked about it plenty of times. We're perfectly suited. Astrid agreed that! We have the same interests, and we want the same things out of life. We were comfortable together.'

'Comfortable isn't romantic!'

'What could be better than finding someone you feel at ease with? Someone you don't need to try with?'

'Because not needing to try is only a short step from not bothering,' said Clara. 'Romance requires a bit of effort, it's true. A little edge, a little frisson of danger. If you want Astrid back, you'll need to step out of your comfort zone and risk showing her how you really feel about her. And I'll give you a little tip for free: telling her that you feel comfortable with her isn't going to win her back!'

She stopped as Ted came weaving his way between the tables. 'Can you do that last bit again?' he said. 'Someone clinked a glass at just the wrong moment.'

'You've been *recording* us?' They looked at him with identical expressions of horror.

'That's generally the idea of filming,' said Ted. 'When we put that little mike on you and gave you the radio mike to put in your pocket, it was so that we could hear you talking,' he explained kindly, as if to two not very bright children. 'See Steve with the camera over there? It's pointed at you because we're filming you. You do understand that means we're taking pictures of you?'

'We didn't think you were ready,' Clara protested.

'I know,' he said, pleased. 'It worked really well. You both looked super natural.'

Simon didn't look natural now. He had pokered up and was regarding Ted with disapproval.

'We were discussing personal matters,' he said severely.

'Oh, don't worry, we can edit out anything personal.' Ted waved away their concerns. 'Visually, it's wonderful. The restaurant, the two of you absorbed in each other...great stuff.'

He beamed at them both. 'So, can you go back to when you were talking about what love is, Clara?'

They did their best to have a neutral discussion, but it felt stilted now. They had managed fine that morning, but there was too much in the air now. Clara kept thinking about Simon as a boy, discovering that his father was flawed. He hadn't said it, but she was certain that he had adored his father and that he had been bereft when he had died.

Ever since then he had been building a wall around his emotions. It would take a lot to bring it down. A very special woman might do it.

But it wouldn't be her.

Clara fiddled with her cutlery, unaccountably dispirited. It was stupid to feel so low. What had she expected? That one kiss would change Simon's view of love?

And, even if it had, what then? They were different in almost every way. Simon might be wrong about love and romance, but he was probably right about the kind of woman he needed. Clara was too noisy, too muddled, too much of a failure. She wouldn't fit into his ruthlessly ordered life any more than he would fit into her somewhat less ordered one. He was no easy-going Matt.

Simon needed Astrid, who was calm and controlled except when she was being swept off her feet by Paolo. Clara suspected Simon was right when he thought Astrid would get tired of the pretty Italian. A toyboy might be fun for a while, but Paolo could never compare to Simon.

No, Astrid would go back to Simon sooner or later. Clara just hoped she recognized just how much love and reassurance Simon needed. Did Astrid understand the desolate boy who was buried deep inside the austere economist?

Clara pulled herself up. What was she thinking? That *she* understood Simon? She had known him for barely twenty-four hours and kissed him once, as a joke. What made her such an expert all of a sudden?

Perhaps she had moved on from Matt after all? That she could even be thinking about Simon this way was a good sign, Clara told herself, but she wasn't going to get carried away. She wanted what she had told Simon: someone special who would love her as she loved him. Someone who would need her and want her, not a substitute or second best, but *her*, Clara.

And that someone wasn't going to be Simon any more than it had been Matt.

So she should stop thinking about his mouth and his hands, and start remembering everything she had said to herself about concentrating on her job.

While she still had one.

'Welcome to Paradise!'

Clara was waiting for Simon when he arrived at St Bonaventure's tiny airport. He walked off the plane looking as crisp and cool as if he was heading into the office instead of stepping into the soupy heat of the tropics.

No board shorts or Hawaiian shirts for Simon Valentine. Instead he wore pale chinos and, in a concession to the heat, a short-sleeved shirt, although he looked as if he would much rather be in a suit.

Clara, who had given herself a stern talking to while she waited for the plane to land, was annoyed to find that her heart gave a great bounce the moment she saw him, momentarily depriving her of breath.

He threw up a hand before she could speak. 'Please, no singalongs from *South Pacific*!'

She was ridiculously glad to see him, grouchy as he was. Forcing her heart back into place, she asked him about his flight. 'I asked them to give you a good seat,' she said, dismayed to find that her voice came out thin and reedy as if there wasn't enough air in her lungs.

Fortunately Simon didn't appear to notice. 'Extremely comfortable,' he said. 'It was very extravagant to send me out first class, though.'

'Don't worry, we didn't pay for first class. Our budget won't stretch *that* far!'

Disturbingly aware of a dangerous fluttery feeling inside her, Clara shifted her sunglasses to her bad hand and pulled the straps of her brightly striped basket back onto her shoulder with her good one. She wasn't supposed to be feeling fluttery. She was supposed to be cool and professional.

'I managed to get you a free upgrade,' she told Simon, horribly afraid that she was babbling. 'We'll just make sure the airline's logo is in the final programme. Ted's outside getting some shots of planes landing now, in fact.'

She stopped, inhaled, made herself slow down.

'Is that all you've brought with you?' she asked, nodding at the neat cabin bag which was all he carried.

'I'm only here for three nights,' Simon pointed out. 'You do realise that it's economic madness for four of us to come all this way just to talk about romance? We could have done that in London!'

'The whole point is that this is another super-romantic place,' said Clara as they headed for the exit. 'You may have resisted the appeal of Paris, but that's a big city, and I'll admit the rain didn't help. But not even you will be able to say that St Bonaventure isn't romantic,' she said. 'Wait till you see where we're staying! It's perfect.'

If only her heart would settle down and her lungs start working properly! It had been two weeks since that trip to Paris, and since then Clara had hardly thought about him at all. Not more than five or six times a day, anyway.

Perhaps she had caught the news once or twice—or maybe a bit more than that, if she was truthful—on the off-chance that Simon would be on, giving one of his concise assessments of the current economic situation, but that was purely for research purposes, Clara reassured herself.

It wasn't because her stomach jerked itself into

a knot every time she remembered that kiss they had shared under the umbrella in Paris, or how it had felt to be held firmly against him in the club while everyone else danced around them.

Not at all.

And if she had been absurdly jittery when she emailed him with details of the trip to St Bonaventure, that was just because it was her job, and she was anxious about getting everything right. She'd never had to organise shooting in so many different locations. Naturally she was nervous!

Simon's reply to her email had been uninformative. *Fine*, was all he had said.

Fine! What was she supposed to make of that?

Well, that was fine by her too. Clara arranged to fly out with Ted and Peter. There was no need to accompany Simon, who was more than capable of getting on a plane by himself and, anyway, they only had one upgrade, so she would have had to sit on her own in cattle class. So it made perfect sense. It was the *professional* thing to do.

Clara had it all worked out. The moment she laid eyes on Simon again, she would wonder what on earth all the jittering had been about. Why, she would think, had she wasted even a minute thinking about him? Her stomach would promptly disentangle itself, that odd fluttery feeling would fade, and she would see the man she had seen at first: uptight, cold, dull.

But it hadn't worked like that. Clara glanced at Simon as he walked easily through the airport terminal with her and saw a self-contained man with a tautly muscled body and a lean, intelligent face. A man with a stern mouth and eyes that seemed to reach right inside her to snare the breath in her lungs. A man with warm hands and a caustic turn of phrase.

He was restrained, not uptight. Guarded, not cold. And when she looked at the hard, exciting angles of his face and remembered the touch of his mouth, dull was the very last word that came to mind.

And he was a man who didn't believe in love and who was looking for an equal. Remember that, Clara?

Outside the air-conditioned terminal, the heat hit them like a blast and they had to screw up their eyes against the glare. Clara put on her sunglasses, glad of the excuse to shield her expression.

She had loved the island as soon as she had

arrived the previous day but now, with Simon beside her, all her senses had intensified and she was acutely aware of the warm breeze lifting her hair and making the palms sway. It carried the scent of the ocean and dried coconut husks from the beach, battling with the airport smell of kerosene and taxi fumes. The sun was warm on her back and the bougainvillaea scrambling over a fence was so intensely pink it hurt the eyes.

And then there was Simon himself, pulling a pair of sunglasses from his shirt pocket but otherwise apparently impervious to the heat. He had nice arms, Clara couldn't help noticing. They were strong with broad wrists and flat, dark hairs on his forearms, and when she found her gaze lingering on his hands, she had to jerk her eyes away.

Ted was waiting for them at the taxi rank. They climbed into a rattling old cab with cracked plastic seats that burnt the back of Clara's legs. She wished she hadn't worn shorts now. She'd picked them because she thought they would be cool.

And flattering, an uncomfortable little voice at the back of her mind reminded her. Her legs were her best feature, and she had wanted to look nice when she met Simon again, admit it.

But if Simon had noticed her legs, he was giving no sign of it.

And that was fine, Clara told herself fiercely. She was here as a professional, not to flaunt her legs in front of the talent.

She cleared her throat. 'It's not far,' she told Simon. 'Once we get to the port, we'll get a sea plane out to the island… Given that we don't have much time, we thought we'd get there as quickly as possible.'

'It would have been even quicker if you'd booked somewhere on the mainland.' Simon was clearly in an astringent mood. 'The sea is the sea, after all.' He was holding onto the roof through the taxi's open window and he looked out at the coconut palms lining the road, making the sunlight flicker as they sped past. Every now and then they got a glimpse of the ocean, a harsh glitter in the midday sun. 'You can't tell me there aren't beautiful beaches here.'

Ted turned round from the passenger seat by the driver. 'Not like Paradise Island,' he promised Simon.

'It's the ultimate romantic hideaway,' said Clara. 'It's gorgeous, isn't it, Ted?'

'I'm sure it's very nice. I'm just questioning the

economic justification for travelling quite so far to make a short segment of the programme.'

Clara rolled her eyes, but she was glad he was being crabby. It made it easier to pretend she wasn't noticing the line of his throat where his open collar lifted in the breeze through the window, that she wasn't burningly conscious of his hand on the seat between them.

The hand she absolutely mustn't lift to see if it felt as warm and firm as she remembered. Clara could feel her fingers twitching with the need to curl around his, and she looped the straps of her basket firmly around them to keep them in place.

'Wait and see,' she promised.

Paradise Island lay in the outskirts of the archipelago that was flung like carelessly discarded jewels in the Indian Ocean west of St Bonaventure itself. Never had an island been better named, in Clara's opinion. It was tiny, set in the middle of a pale, pale green lagoon, with the dark blue ocean surging against the reef beyond. The water was so clear they could see the reflection of the sea plane on the sandy bottom as they flew over the lagoon.

There was a central area with a bar and restaurant, but the guests stayed in individual wooden huts, simply but luxuriously decorated, each opening out onto the beach. Simon and the MediaOchre crew all had a hut to themselves in the same part of the beach.

'We're all the same,' Clara told him. 'There's no need to swap rooms this time.'

By the time Simon had washed and changed into shorts and a loose shirt, the glare had gone from the sky, and he went out to find Clara.

She was sitting at the end of a long wooden dock that speared out into the lagoon, etched against the horizon in blocks of vibrant colour. Green shorts, a turquoise-blue sleeveless top. The neon-green cast on her arm that clashed horribly with both. It was so much part of Clara now that Simon had almost stopped noticing it. Her hair hung loose to her shoulders, pulled back by the sunglasses perched on top of her head, and her legs dangled in the water.

At the sound of his footsteps, she looked over her shoulder and smiled.

'Go on,' she said as he sat down next to her and let his own feet hang in the translucent water. It was very quiet, with just the gentle slap of the lagoon against the dock and the faint boom of the ocean beyond the reef. 'Admit it,' she said. 'This is paradise.'

'It's very attractive,' he conceded.

'Attractive?' Clara threw up her hands in disbelief. 'It's more than just attractive. It's incredibly, amazingly, stunningly beautiful!'

Simon had been watching the way the sunlight threw wavering reflections over their legs, but he turned his head to look at her then.

He liked the fact that Clara was tall. Their eyes were almost at the same level. Hers were brown and indignant, with the tilting lashes he had remembered, and her skin had already picked up a glow from the sun.

His gaze dropped to the warm, curving mouth that he had been unable to banish from his mind. If he were a more fanciful man, Simon would have said that mouth had haunted him since their return from Paris, but how could it do that? It was just a mouth after all, and that was just a throat, just a chin, just a cheek with a sweet curve to it. Taken one by one, there was nothing special about any of them.

But, put together, they made Clara. Warm, humorous Clara, forever on the point of breaking into a song or a smile.

Simon examined her face. It reminded him of a picture his mother had showed him when he was a small boy. If you looked at it one way, you saw a profile of an old woman, but when you looked again, you could see an elegant young one instead. Clara was like that. Sometimes she was a perfectly ordinary young woman, but if you blinked and looked again, suddenly she was gorgeous.

His gaze came back to hers. 'All right,' he said, without looking at the view. 'It's beautiful.'

Too late, he realised that he had made a mistake. Why was he looking into her eyes? Now he was pinioned, trapped, unable to look away, while the silence stretched around them and time seemed to stop and there was nothing but that moment. Nothing but the hard wooden dock beneath his thighs, nothing but the silky warmth of the water against his skin.

And Clara's gaze tangled with his, the indignation fading to an expression Simon couldn't identify but that made his throat tighten painfully all the same.

Deep inside him, Simon felt something inside him unlock, so clearly that he could almost hear it click, and the sensation was so vivid it jerked him back to reality.

Because unlocking was a bad idea. A bad, bad idea. Unlocking was the first step to opening up, to letting go, and letting go meant losing control. Simon's heart was actually thumping in alarm at the prospect, and he dragged his eyes away from Clara's with an effort.

He found himself staring at her legs instead, but that wasn't any better. She had great legs, long and bare and smooth. Simon calculated that he would only have to shift an inch or so for his left thigh to be touching her right one, for their shoulders to touch. And, if that happened, it would be so easy to slide a hand under her hair and pull her towards him…

The impulse was so strong that it seemed to Simon that Clara was a powerful magnet, tugging him towards her. The effort of resistance had his heart going like a steam engine, and it was only by sheer force of will that he managed to wrench his gaze away from her legs. He stared out to where a cat's paw of wind ruffled the surface of the lagoon, sending shivers across the pure green water, until he felt his pulse settle and whatever it was that had unlocked had clicked firmly back in place.

They sat on the end of the dock, carefully watching the horizon, carefully not touching, while the silence yawned around them.

Simon cleared his throat. 'How's the wrist?' he managed to ask at last, but his tongue felt thick and unwieldy in his mouth, and he was excruciatingly aware of how close Clara was. An inch, two, that was all it would take. He swallowed hard. 'I thought you'd be out of the cast by now.'

'Another couple of weeks.' The words came out oddly squeezed as she lifted the cast to show him. 'It's fine, though. I hardly notice I've got it on most of the time.

'It's a pain here, though,' she said, sounding more like herself, as if she had shifted her voice down a gear. 'I can't swim or snorkel, and I have to wear a plastic bag on the beach to stop sand getting down my cast. I tried sitting in the water with my arm in the air, but I look a complete idiot,' she said glumly.

'It's the mark of a heroine, remember?' said Simon and her mouth pulled down at the corners.

'Frankly, I'd rather be a coward and be able to swim.'

'But then you wouldn't have been able to black-mail me into being here.'

'True.' Clara sat up a bit straighter and swung her legs in the water, making the reflections rock wildly. 'So, tell me, what have you been doing since Paris?'

'Working.'

'Have you seen Astrid?'

'Yes,' he said reluctantly.

'And?'

'And what?'

'And did you sweep her off her feet? Were you romantic? Did you win her back from Paolo?'

Simon presumed she was joking. 'We went out for a drink,' he said. 'Astrid seemed…concerned.'

'Concerned? What about?'

'About you.'

Clara's feet stopped swinging and she turned to stare at him. *'Me?'*

Simon didn't want to spoil the mood, but she probably ought to know. 'Apparently Stella spread a few nasty rumours after she got back from Paris,' he said, picking his way carefully.

'What kind of rumours?'

'I thought you might have heard.'

'No.' Clara fixed him with those bright brown eyes. 'What did she say?'

'Stupid things.' Simon shifted uneasily. 'How you had thrown yourself at me and we'd spent the entire time in bed and refused to turn up for filming or do any work at all.'

Her eyes widened. *'What?'*

'It's all rubbish, of course,' he said, 'but I gather Stella was quite persuasive, and I've always been so straight-laced it was a story everyone enjoyed, so it's been doing the rounds.'

'You mean people really think that...*you*...and *me*...?' She pointed at him and then at herself. 'How ridiculous!' she said unevenly when he nodded.

'Quite.'

Her gaze slid away from his.

'But Astrid can't have been concerned about *that*?' she said after a moment. 'She must know you better than that!'

'I think she was afraid I'd gone off the rails,' said Simon.

There was a pause. Clara glanced at him, clearly thinking that it was impossible to imagine anyone more firmly *on* the rails and under control, and when she looked away he saw her bite her cheeks to hide a smile.

'Go ahead,' he said, resigned. 'Laugh.'

CHAPTER EIGHT

CLARA'S peal of laughter rang out across the lagoon, and Simon felt an answering smile twitch at the corners of his mouth.

For some reason, that broke the intensity of the mood and lessened the constraint between them. Clara pulled one foot out of the water so that she could hug her knee and half turn towards him, amusement still dancing in her eyes.

'I hope you were able to reassure her!'

'I think so.' Simon squinted out at the reef, remembering the conversation. 'She was in a strange mood, though. She kept going on about you and how "vulnerable" I was.'

'That's because she's jealous!' Clara gave him a *duh* look. 'I told you she would be. It's a good sign.' She flicked her hair back over her shoulder with her good hand. 'What did you say?'

'Nothing. She's still with Paolo.' Simon had wondered whether Astrid might be jealous himself. She had been very conciliating, almost as if she were waiting for him to ask her to come back.

It would have been easy, and he *had* thought about it, but somehow the words hadn't come. Simon still didn't really know why he had held back. He had spent a lot of time since Paris reminding himself how perfectly he and Astrid were suited, but when she was right in front of him, he felt...nothing.

But after she had gone he had been exasperated with himself. That was Clara's fault, he had decided. It would never have occurred to him to worry about feelings until he had met her.

'You don't want to play it too cool,' Clara warned. 'You could send her some flowers when you get home. Ask her to dinner and tell her you missed her. Or say you'd like to take her to Paris. If she really is jealous, she'll want to come back, but you have to show her that you've changed and that you really want her.'

'I'd forgotten that you were the great romance expert,' said Simon, a faint edge to his voice. She seemed absolutely determined to get him back with Astrid, and the thought left him vaguely disgruntled.

Clara was leaning forward, her eyes intent. 'If

Astrid gets a glimpse of passion from you, she'll drop Paolo like a shot,' she told him. 'You can have your nice comfortable life back. Surely that's worth a romantic gesture or two?'

'I suppose so.' Simon could hear the doubt in his own voice.

'That is what you want, isn't it?'

'Of course,' he said, but Clara had noticed that tiny hesitation, he could tell.

It *was* what he wanted, Simon insisted to himself. He'd had much the same conversation with his mother only the week before, and he'd been absolutely sure then.

Frances had wanted to know all about Paris, and how he had got on with Clara. Simon had told her everything—oh, not about the kiss, but everything else. She knew about the way Clara danced, about her exasperating habit of humming under her breath, and the leaps of logic that left Simon wanting to tear his hair out.

'She sounds perfect for you,' Frances had said and Simon had stared at her, convinced that she had finally taken leave of her senses.

'*Astrid* is perfect for me,' he'd corrected her, but his mother only looked at him pityingly.

'For such a clever man, darling, you can be very

stupid,' she had said. Simon was still puzzling over that one.

Now he sat on the dock beside Clara and made himself remember everything he liked about Astrid. Her clear mind. Her poise and elegance. The way she had never pushed him. She understood his work, understood how he thought.

No, they were perfect for each other.

'Of course that's what I want,' he said more firmly.

They were a smaller crew this time. Ted was acting as cameraman as well as director to save money, and Peter was doing sound again. Later that evening, Clara and Simon walked over to join them in the restaurant.

'I'm surprised Roland isn't here,' said Simon, distracted by the way she looked, with her shoulders bare and a frangipani flower in her hair. A sarong patterned with hibiscus flowers was wrapped around her hips, and the night was so warm all she wore with it was a strappy top and spangled flip-flops.

'He's wheeling and dealing,' said Clara. 'That's what he really likes doing. He calls himself executive producer, but he's not really interested in the practicalities. He only came to Paris to make sure you and Stella were happy—and we know how well *that* turned out,' she added ruefully.

'Has he forgiven you yet?'

'Just about.' Clara made a face. 'Ted seems to have convinced him that it's going to work fine without Stella, but I've been keeping a low profile. I can't afford to alienate Roland again. He promised me a chance at producing if this programme was a success, but I suspect I can wave goodbye to that for now. It's a shame, as I'm not likely to get a better chance.'

Catching herself up on a sigh, she smiled at Simon. 'Never mind. I'm not going to think about that now. I'm lucky I've still got a job at all, frankly.'

'It's not unreasonable to want financial security,' said Simon, who was having some trouble keeping his attention on economic realities when those hibiscus-clad hips were swaying.

'Simon, we're on Paradise Island,' said Clara as they climbed the steps to the restaurant. Candlelit tables were set out over a large covered deck area, decorated with plants and huge pots and open on all sides.

'This is not the place to think about practicalities,' she said. 'This is the place to think about how warm the night is, how starry it is. Look at how many honeymooning couples there are here. This is a place made for romance, not reality.'

'We're not here for romance, though, are we?' Simon heard himself say, and then regretted it when a guarded look flickered across her face before she pinned on a smile.

'No, of course not,' she said brightly, 'but that doesn't mean we can't enjoy the rest of it.' She waved her good arm in an all-encompassing gesture. 'The tropical night, the quiet...oh, and the food, of course.' Catching sight of Ted and Peter on the far side of the restaurant, she waved and set off through the tables. 'I can recommend the prawns,' she said over her shoulder. 'They were to die for last night.'

An uneasy feeling in her stomach woke Clara in the early hours. For a while she lay hoping it would go away, until unease became urgency, and then panic. She only just made it to the luxury bathroom in time.

When Simon knocked on her door that morning, she could barely lift her head off the pillow to croak, 'Come in.'

'Clara?' He was barely through the door before she had to make another humiliating dash to the bathroom.

It was Simon who produced a bucket, Simon who broke the news to Ted and Peter that there was no way Clara could stand in front of a camera, Simon who made sure that she had fresh water to drink and then held her head as she threw it all up again.

Having disposed of the contents, he came back with a wet flannel so that she could wipe her face.

'Is this when I start singing about your favourite things? Or what about a spoonful of sugar?'

Clara dragged the flannel over her face. Even that was an effort. Her hair was tangled and she strongly suspected that she was an unattractive shade somewhere between grey and green. That was how she felt, anyway.

'I can't believe you're making fun of me when I'm dying.'

Simon smiled. 'I don't think it's quite as bad as that. You've obviously had a nasty little bout of food poisoning. One of those prawns you were raving about last night, probably.'

'Uuurrrgghhh…' Clara clapped one hand to

her mouth, the other to her stomach at the very thought of prawns.

'You'll be fine,' said Simon soothingly. 'It just needs to work its way through your system. Twenty-four hours and you'll be right as rain.'

Twenty-four hours! She struggled up on her pillows. 'I have to get up. We've only got today and tomorrow morning.'

The words were barely out of her mouth before the cramps hit her again. Obligingly, Simon passed the bucket.

'Oh, God, Ted's going to kill me,' she moaned when she could.

'He's fine. I'm going to do a few pieces to camera about the economic exploitation of these islands and what happens to indigenous populations when tourism takes over.'

'That sounds like fun,' Clara managed, still hanging over the bucket.

'We'll fit you in later when you're on your feet.'

Clara just groaned. 'Go away and let me die in peace.'

Simon smiled and smoothed some stray strands of hair from her clammy forehead. 'I'll come back and check on you later.'

So Clara lay and, between vile episodes in the

bathroom and hanging over the bucket, alternated between wanting to die and squirming with humiliation whenever she remembered how kind Simon had been. Ted, never the most stoical of friends, had only managed to blow a kiss from the doorway before blenching and departing hastily, but Simon had been infinitely reassuring. Clara was torn, partly longing for his visits, and partly horrified that he had seen her at her absolute worst.

'I must look terrible,' she said on his last visit. She hadn't been sick for an hour and was hoping the worst was over.

'You're feeling better if you care what you look like,' he pointed out. 'Do you think you could manage a shower?'

Clara sat up cautiously. 'Does Ted want me now?'

'Don't fret. It's all decided. There's time to do your bits tomorrow before the flight back.'

'I can't believe I've wasted half my time here throwing up!' she said, slumping back against her pillows.

'It's all been terribly romantic, I know,' said Simon, then ducked as she threw a pillow at him.

'You're definitely on the mend,' he said. 'You'll feel even better if you have a shower.'

Clara did. She had a shower, washed her hair and brushed her teeth vigorously, but she was so weak she had to keep sitting down. Eventually, she managed to drag on a T-shirt and another sarong, and made her way on wobbly legs to the hut's little verandah.

Simon was coming along the sandy path from the beach, silhouetted against the setting sun. He stopped at the bottom of her steps and looked up at her, the stern features relaxing into a smile.

'You're up.'

The hollow feeling in her stomach was entirely due to food poisoning, Clara told herself. That was the only reason her knees were so weak that she had to hold onto the door frame for support.

'I couldn't stay inside any longer.'

'How are you feeling?'

She patted her stomach cautiously. 'Empty. Thinner.'

'Can you manage a little walk?'

In the end, she could only make it as far as the beach, which wasn't very far at all, but it was worth it when she was sitting on the soft sand, still warm after a day under the tropical sun.

Clara dug her bare toes into it and sighed contentedly. 'It's beautiful.'

Simon sat beside her and together they watched the sun set in a spectacular flush of orange and red. Further down the beach, a honeymoon couple wandered hand in hand along the edge of the lagoon. Clara remembered doing that with Matt on a beach in Greece. Funny how the memory didn't hurt any more.

Her eyes followed the couple as she absently picked up handfuls of the fine sand and let it trickle through her fingers, enjoying its fineness. Beside her Simon was lying back on his elbows, his ankles crossed. He looked cool and contained, and her mouth dried with wanting him.

What would it be like if they were on their honeymoon, like the couple further down the beach? If they loved each other and were starting their life together? If she could reach out and touch him whenever she wanted, and know that he would smile and pull her down to him? If Simon had lowered his guard and let himself love?

A lot of ifs there, Clara realised with a sigh, and face it, none of them was going to happen.

And, anyway, some honeymoon it would have been with her chucking up all day.

She was getting as bad as Simon, she thought wryly, puncturing a lovely dream with reality.

The sky was crimson, fading to purple and then dark, and out of nowhere came the thought that romance was like the sunset, a flush of something amazing and wonderful that faded to mundane reality.

A tiny crease between her brows, Clara lay back beside Simon, who had stretched out flat and was looking up at the fringed palm leaves that stirred and rustled in the warm breeze.

'What's the matter?' asked Simon.

'Nothing.'

'You keep sighing.'

Clara was ruffled. 'I sighed *once*!'

'Twice. You sighed just now when you lay down.' He turned his head to look at her. 'I'd have thought you'd have been in heaven.'

'I am,' she said with a shade of defiance. 'This is about as romantic as it gets.'

The tropical night had fallen with dizzying suddenness. Clara was agonisingly aware of Simon's dark, solid bulk next to her on the sand. It was as if the night had closed around them, sealing them in a tiny bubble that was slowly leaking oxygen.

She found that she was breathing very carefully so as not to use it up too quickly.

Desperately, she made herself focus on the night, on the soft sigh of the lagoon and the whirr of the cicadas, on the silkiness of the sand under her toes and the scent of the frangipani drifting in the warm air. Closing her eyes, she began to hum softly.

'What's that?' asked Simon lazily. 'Another gem from *The Sound of Music*?'

Clara opened her eyes and stared at him in disbelief. 'It's from *South Pacific*. Even you must know *Some Enchanted Evening*!'

He made a non-committal sound, and she shook her head at the depths of his ignorance as she sang the first few lines.

'It *is* an enchanted evening,' she said, heaving a sigh. 'Can't you feel it? A deserted beach, a starry night, the only sound the hot wind soughing through the palm trees...'

'I can hear a generator, too,' Simon pointed out.

Clara clicked her tongue, provoked. 'You're just being difficult. I don't believe you can't understand how fabulously romantic this all is. It's a perfect tropical night, and Paradise Island is exactly what I imagined a coral island to be like. I don't see how you could possibly improve it.'

'Oh, surely it can get better than this,' he said.

'I don't see how.'

Simon propped himself up on one elbow so that he could look down at her. 'We could kiss.'

He made the suggestion so casually that Clara wasn't sure that she had heard properly.

The little breath that was left in her lungs leaked away. 'Do you think that's a good idea?'

'Well, according to your theory it would make it even more romantic, wouldn't it?'

'It might,' she agreed unevenly, and Simon's teeth gleamed in the darkness as he smiled.

'It worked in Paris in the rain.'

'Hmm…that's true.'

This was probably a big mistake. Hadn't she spent the last two weeks talking herself out of being attracted to Simon? Didn't she *know* that it could never work with him?

But wouldn't it feel good? And shouldn't it be her mission to convince him that romance was possible, even if it was just a kiss on a tropical beach in the dark?

Just one kiss. What harm could it do? Neither of them was committed to anyone else.

And it would feel so good…

'If this evening is as enchanted as you say, it seems a waste not to make the most of it, don't you think?' Simon lifted her hair and smoothed it behind her ear, letting his fingers linger against her cheek, making her tremble with need.

'Rude not to,' she agreed raggedly.

'We could think of it as a useful comparative exercise,' he said, leaning over her. 'Which is more romantic? To kiss in Paris when you're soaked to the skin or on a tropical beach when one of you has spent the day groaning over a bucket?'

'Ugh, don't mention food poisoning,' said Clara, but she was fingering the bottom of his shirt and made no effort to move away as Simon lowered his head.

'The thing is, I'm a rational man,' he said. 'I can't make a decision based on feelings. I need to test the empirical evidence before I make up my mind as to which is the more romantic place.'

Clara's toes were curling in the sand and, without quite meaning to, she lifted her hands to his shoulders. 'Good point,' she said.

Very slowly, Simon lowered his head until his mouth was almost—*almost* touching hers. 'So shall we test the hypothesis?'

'I suppose so,' she managed unsteadily. 'Just in the interests of scientific research.'

'Naturally,' said Simon. She felt his mouth curve in a smile. It fitted hers perfectly, and she realised that she was smiling too.

At the back of her mind, a small, sensible part of Clara had retained just enough grip on reality to think *uh-oh, perhaps this isn't such a good idea after all,* and was frantically waving a warning flag, but she frowned it down.

How could it not be a good idea when Simon was pressing her into the sand and his body was warm and wonderfully solid? When his competent hands were unwinding her sarong and his kisses swamped her with pleasure? When there was only the distant boom of surf against the reef and the lap of the lagoon on the shore and the warm darkness that wrapped itself around them like a caress?

When it really *was* an enchanted evening?

So Clara turned her mental back on that warning flag and kissed Simon back. She moved her hands down his flanks to slide them under his shirt, hissing in a breath at the feel of his bare skin. His back was broad and smooth and powerfully muscled beneath her palms, and she arched into the sand with a gasp as his lips travelled down the side of her neck to the curve of her shoulder in a trail of wicked pleasure.

How could this possibly be a bad idea? Clara abandoned herself without regret to the honeyed delight of feeling him, touching him, *tasting* him.

To the bone-melting pleasure that dissolved in its turn to a dizzying rush of heat.

To the insistent pulse of excitement as his hungry hands unlocked her, as his mouth drove her to the pitch of need and she clutched at him, loving his hard weight on her, fingering the bumps in his spine, smiling as he flexed in response.

'This is madness,' Simon mumbled against her throat.

'I know.' Her arms slid around his neck, pulled him closer. 'Madness, I know.'

And then they sank back down into the glorious, giddy heat once more.

Mouths, hands. Touch, feel. Gasp, sigh.

Kiss. Kiss, kiss, kiss.

Time slowed and swirled. 'We should stop,' Simon muttered, not stopping.

The warning flag struggled to the top of Clara's consciousness once more, waving exhaustedly. 'Probably,' she agreed reluctantly.

Simon drew a long steadying breath. Levering himself off her, he rolled back onto the sand beside her. For a while they lay there, letting their breathing quieten.

Having caught her attention at last, the sensible part of Clara's mind was firmly back in charge. It had been a wonderful kiss, but she mustn't read too much into it. Simon Valentine might kiss better than any other man she had ever kissed, but he was still a man who didn't believe in love.

He might desire her now, on the beach, in the dark, skimpily dressed—he was a guy, after all—but she wasn't the one he really wanted.

Clara made herself remember everything he'd told her about Astrid in Paris. *I don't want anyone else*, he had said. Astrid was perfect for Simon, he had said so and, no matter how much he might resist the idea, Clara thought he probably did love Astrid. As much as he dared to, anyway.

And Clara wasn't playing second best again. She wasn't going to be a substitute, a temporary replacement, until the one he really wanted became available. She had been there with Matt, and she wasn't going there again. It had hurt too much.

So she would treat it lightly, the way she had learnt to do. It was easier that way.

'So what did you decide?' she asked Simon.

'Decide?' He sounded distracted.

'Is the beach more romantic than Paris?'

A tiny, tiny pause. 'It's definitely more convenient. It's dark and dry and we're lying down for a start, so yes, I vote for the tropical paradise.'

His voice was back to its normal astringency by then, but his hand found Clara's in the darkness, and her throat tightened at the intimacy of their entangled fingers.

'It's easy to get carried away in the dark,' she agreed after a moment. 'I knew you wouldn't be able to resist the romance of it all.'

'Is it romance or is it physical attraction?'

'It's probably a bit of both,' said Clara, hearing the wariness in his voice. 'But you don't need to panic. I'm not talking about love. I'm talking about the way a place like this helps you let down your barriers.'

It was true, thought Simon. He had lowered his guard, but was that because of the darkness and heat and the scents of the tropical night, or was it because of Clara herself?

I'm a rational man, he had told her, but reason

had evaporated the moment his mouth had touched hers and he had succumbed to the wild sweetness. The world had swung round them, but there at its centre, holding everything steady, had been Clara.

Now he lay, his fingers entwined with hers, and felt the earth turning beneath them, and he felt exposed and vulnerable and yet as if everything was in its right place.

'I know you don't do love,' said Clara.

That was true, too.

Simon wondered what he was feeling now. Desire, certainly, but beyond that, something new, something disturbing, was coiling around his heart. Something that made him shift uneasily on the sand.

'I don't like feeling out of control.'

'I know you don't. And you don't need to worry,' she told him, sounding remarkably cheerful, Simon couldn't help noticing.

How could she kiss like that, and then bounce straight back to normal? It wasn't natural. Wasn't her blood still pounding? Wasn't her body still clenched with desire?

'I'm not falling in love with someone who can't

love me back completely,' she said. 'So we both know where we are.'

He ought to be glad she was so businesslike about it. He *was* glad. It was just… Well, Simon didn't *know* what it was. He just knew he felt edgy and faintly aggrieved, and how irrational was *that*?

I'm a rational man. Hah!

Disentangling her fingers, Clara sat up and tried to wrap her sarong around her once more. The sarong he had unwound so efficiently so that he could smooth his hand down her thigh and stroke the inside of her knee.

Simon wrenched his mind back on track and sat up as well, resting his wrists on his bent knees.

The sarong was hopelessly twisted, and Clara had given up. She was brushing sand off herself instead.

'Anyway,' she said, 'I know it's Astrid you want, so there's no danger of either of us misinterpreting what just happened.' She glanced at him, trying to gauge his reaction. 'That doesn't mean I didn't enjoy it.'

If Clara the great romantic could be casual about a kiss that had shaken him to his core, *he* certainly could!

'I enjoyed it too,' he said.

'Perhaps we should test the hypothesis again in Scotland,' Clara suggested tentatively.

'Scotland?'

'That's going to be the last segment of the programme. We'll have done Paris, and a tropical paradise. An isolated cottage in the Highlands is another kind of romantic place, and it'll be the perfect contrast to the other two.'

'Aren't the Highlands cold and wet and plagued with midges? What's romantic about that?'

'There won't be any midges when we go,' said Clara firmly, omitting the cold and wet issue. 'It'll be wonderful.'

'When have you been to the Highlands?'

'Never, as it happens, but I know I'm going to love it. It'll be *elemental*.' She hugged herself at the thought. 'Wild hills, the mist on the heather, the rain lashing at the windows…'

Simon sighed, but actually he was feeling better. More himself. This was Clara in normal, exasperatingly illogical mode, and he could deal with that much better than he could with the Clara whose softness and warmth made his mind reel.

'What is it with you and rain? Didn't we have enough rain in Paris?'

'It'll be different in Scotland. You expect it there.'

Above their heads, the palms rustled in the breeze and somewhere in the darkness there was a thud as a coconut dropped into the sand.

Bizarre to be having a conversation about hills and cold and rain on this tropical beach. Scotland was another world—a world where things would be back to normal, Simon hoped. Where he would be back in control. Where there would be no warmth and languid nights to seduce him into lowering his guard once more.

'When are we going up there?' he asked.

'The end of March, if that works for you,' said Clara, head bent over her knees as she combed the sand from her hair with her fingers.

'And you think we should have another kiss there?'

She peered up at him through her hair. 'Just for comparative purposes, of course.'

'Of course.'

'And if you're not back with Astrid,' she added.

'Of course,' he said again, distracted by the sweet curve of the nape of her neck. He made himself look away. If it was anything like the kiss they'd just shared, it would be worth all that lashing rain. 'I'll look forward to it.'

'When you said it was isolated, you really meant it.'

Simon rested his arms on the steering wheel and peered through the windscreen at the white-washed cottage lit by the beam of his headlights.

They had been driving along a bumpy track in the pitch-dark for what seemed like hours. The last sign of human habitation was miles behind them, and it was a long time since either of them had been able to get a signal on their mobile phones.

And it was starting to snow.

Excellent.

When Simon turned off the engine, all that could be heard was the keen of the wind screaming down from the mountains that were shrouded in the snowy darkness. It buffeted the car, making it rock slightly. The prospect of getting out into it and fighting their way to the dark cottage was uninviting, to say the least.

Clara eyed the cottage doubtfully. 'It looked nicer on the Internet.'

'The snow is a nice touch.' Simon allowed

sarcasm to lace his voice. It had been a very long drive. 'You've certainly covered a range of weather in this programme of yours.'

'Well, getting snowed in is always romantic.' Clara slid a glance at Simon, wondering if it would be pushing things too far to sing *Always Look on the Bright Side of Life*, and deciding against it after one look at the set of his jaw.

'It's a pity it's not Christmas,' she said instead. 'That really *would* have been romantic.'

Simon was looking sceptical. 'We just need the others to arrive,' she said, trying to cheer him up. Ted, Peter and Steve were driving up in a van loaded with equipment and the food Clara had bought the day before. 'I did a big shop so there'll be lots of nice things to eat. We'll make a fire. It'll be cosy.'

'You're doing Julie Andrews again,' he said sourly. 'Stop it.'

Simon had elected to drive his own car north, obviously not trusting Clara's driving, in spite of the fact that her wrist was out of its cast at last. She had to admit that it was more comfortable than a hired car, and certainly than the van would have been.

He was a good driver, fast and competent, his

hands very steady on the steering wheel, but it had still been a very long drive. Clara had entertained herself—and Simon, she had thought—with a repertoire of all the songs from the musicals she knew until he had told her that he would put her in the boot if he had to hear one more.

'That damn tune about the lonely goatherd is in my head now,' he growled.

'You should sing along,' said Clara. 'That'll let it out of your head.'

One look from Simon was enough to tell her what he thought of *that* suggestion.

Fine. She wouldn't sing then. After a while, without really being aware of it, she began humming under her breath.

'Stop buzzing!' said Simon, exasperated. 'Why can't you just sit quietly and look at the scenery?'

'I don't like silence.' Clara hunched a sullen shoulder.

It had been nearly a month since that kiss on St Bonaventure, and she had done her best to put it out of her mind, but she couldn't help remembering that they had agreed to kiss again in Scotland.

Just as a light-hearted test.

I'll look forward to it, Simon had said. Every time Clara thought of it, which was more often than she wanted, anticipation shivered down her spine and clenched her entrails.

It was madness, they had agreed on that beach, and it still was. This was the last time she and Simon would meet. Once the filming was over, their lives would go their separate ways for good. Ted would edit her out of the film, so they wouldn't even stay together digitally. How symbolic was that?

She and Simon had nothing whatsoever in common, Clara knew that, but still she couldn't stop the excitement buzzing under her skin when she thought about him, and the moment she had seen him again it was as if a light had been switched on inside her.

CHAPTER NINE

IT DIDN'T make sense. Yes, he was a fantastic kisser, but he was also cross, critical and infuriatingly unromantic. He didn't sing, couldn't dance. He was her very own Captain von Trapp, in fact.

Which made Astrid the Baroness.

Who, let's face it, had much nicer frocks and in reality would have made him a much more suitable wife than a guitar-strumming nun.

Clara suppressed a sigh. 'I suppose Astrid behaves perfectly in the car?'

'At least she can sit still for more than a minute at a time, and doesn't subject me to the complete works of Andrew Lloyd Webber and Rodgers and Hammerstein!'

Clara didn't normally like long car journeys, which did indeed involve too much sitting still for her liking, but she hadn't been bored. How could she be bored when being with Simon made her feel so alive? Every one of her senses was on high alert, and she was intensely aware of the beating of her own heart.

Of the smell of the leather seats and the smoothness of the glossy wood trim, of the length of Simon's thigh, and the dashboard lights which threw a muted glow over his features, catching the line of his nose and the set of his mouth in a way that dried the breath in Clara's throat whenever she looked at it.

When not providing Simon with a free cabaret—which he hadn't appreciated at all—Clara had spent the journey curled up in her seat, half-turned towards him, and they had talked and argued their way all the way up the motorway.

Simon was one of those drivers who hated breaking the momentum of their journey and, in spite of constant lobbying for a proper meal, Clara had barely been allowed the occasional brief loo stop. She had a sandwich and a packet of crisps that earned her a ticking off for dropping crumbs all over his car, but now they were there and she was starving.

'Well, let's see what it's like inside,' she said, digging in her bag for the key they had picked up a lifetime earlier. 'I'm sure it'll be fine once we've got the kettle on and a fire going.'

She had to push hard to open the car door. The wind snatched at her hair and spat snow into her eyes as soon as she got out, and she made a bolt for the cottage. She was shivering so much she couldn't get the key in the lock.

'What are you doing?' Simon had to raise his voice above the howling wind and, even fumbling around in the dark with the snow swirling around them, she was acutely aware of his body behind her.

'My hands are cold,' she yelled back.

'Let me do it.' His fingers were warm and sure as he reached out and took the key from her, and for an instant Clara was transported back to Paradise Island and his hand on her thigh, on the back of her knee.

The rush of heat warmed her as Simon opened the door without any difficulty and groped around for a light switch.

'Ah,' he said as he encountered one and clicked it on.

Nothing.

He switched it off and then on again. Still nothing.

'What's the matter?' said Clara, who was shivering again after that brief, welcome spurt of warmth.

'No power.'

'Ohmigod...' Clara's dream of a cosy cottage was rapidly fading.

'Perhaps it's just the bulb.'

But when Simon located another switch, that didn't work either.

'Now what?' Clara said as he cursed.

'See if you can find the fuse box.'

Muttering under his breath, Simon fought his way back through the wind and snow to the car and stomped back with a torch.

Clara was very glad of his competence. She certainly wouldn't have known what to do. Tasked with holding the torch, she huddled behind him, pulling her sleeves down over her hands, while he examined the fuse box.

'I can't see if you wave the torch around like that,' Simon said irritably.

'It's cold,' she grumbled, but she eased her fingers out of her jumper to hold the torch steadier.

Simon straightened, and they were suddenly standing very close. Clara took an instinctive step back, which seemed a better idea than throwing herself at his chest, which was what she really wanted to do.

'The fuses are OK,' he said, taking the torch from her briskly and playing it around the room. 'That means the power is out further down the line. There's nothing we can do about that.'

Clara hugged her arms together in dismay. 'What are we going to do? This is a nightmare.'

'You were the one who thought an isolated cottage would be romantic,' he reminded her.

True, she had.

'It'll be cosy, you said,' Simon added maliciously. 'It'll be wonderful, you said. It'll be *elemental*.'

'We'll make it cosy,' said Clara, pulling herself together. 'There must be a fire. Let's have that torch. Look, there,' she said in relief, spotting a mantelpiece.

'That's something,' grunted Simon. 'You get it going and I'll bring our stuff in from the car.'

Fortunately the fire had been laid, and Clara found some matches. They were the first tenants of the year, the agent had told them, and the matches were rather damp, but she eventually managed to get one to light. She was shivering so hard by then that the match nearly went out as she held it to the paper with a shaking hand, but at last a tiny flame caught the edge of the paper.

Clara watched it anxiously as it wavered, then steadied. Puffing out a sigh of relief, she sat back on her heels, holding out her hands to the fire as it crackled into life. Now she knew how cavemen must have felt. There was something infinitely comforting about the leaping flames in the darkness.

Simon pushed the door shut with his foot and dumped their things by the door while he brushed the snow from his jacket. They didn't have much with them. It had seemed silly to load up the car when the van could bring everything more easily.

Which might have been a mistake.

'I'm starving,' said Clara, switching off the torch to save the battery. 'I hope Ted and the others arrive soon. They've got all the food.'

'We won't be able to cook it,' Simon pointed out as he dropped wearily into a chair on one side of the fire and stretched out his legs to the flames. 'The oven's electric.'

Clara's shoulders slumped. She had been fantasising about the piece of lamb she'd bought to roast.

'There's bread and cheese.' She perked up a

little as she remembered what else they could eat. 'Crisps, olives…oh, and wine, of course.'

She sighed. 'I must stop thinking about it. I'm drooling! I can't even find out how far away they are.' Just in case a signal had miraculously winkled its way through the mountains, she dug her phone out of her bag. It was still blank, but she did find the end of a packet of mints that she had forgotten was there.

'Want a mint?' she offered Simon.

'Why not save them until we're desperate?'

'I'm desperate now!' But she put the mints back, and got to her feet and picked up the torch.

'I'm going to see if there's anything in the kitchen.'

'Don't waste the battery,' Simon warned.

'I'll be quick.'

It was too cold to be away from the fire for too long anyway. Clara hunted through the kitchen cupboards but could only find some old instant coffee and two cans of kidney beans.

'No can opener either,' she reported glumly when she was huddled back in front of the fire. 'We'd better eke out those mints or we'll be reduced to gnawing our own limbs.'

Simon added a log to the fire and poked it into

place. 'That's right,' he said. 'A quick step from a twinge of hunger to cannibalism. Why am I even surprised?' He threw himself back into the chair. 'Do you ever react moderately to anything?'

'I don't need to be moderate when you're sitting there being moderate enough for ten of us!' said Clara pettishly.

'There's no point in me doing drama when you're sitting there being dramatic enough for twenty!'

There was an unpleasant silence, and then Clara sighed. 'I'm sorry,' she said. 'I'm just cross because this is turning into a nightmare.'

Dispirited, she looked around the cottage. It was difficult to make out much in the firelight, but she didn't hold out much hope of the charming, cosy décor she had imagined. There were some bulky pieces of furniture, most of it dating from the Seventies to judge by the knobbly material on the three-piece suite in front of the fireplace, and a musty smell pervaded everything.

'You're right,' she told Simon miserably. 'It's not romantic at all. It's awful. Maybe I've got it all wrong.'

Simon sat up in mock alarm. 'That's not like

you! Isn't there some song you can sing to make you feel better?'

'I don't feel like singing,' said Clara, settling herself with her back against the sofa.

'Now you've really got me worried,' he said, only half-joking.

She tucked her hair behind her ears and forced herself to face up to the truth.

'All these romantic situations have turned out to be disasters,' she said in a hollow voice. 'Pouring in Paris, food poisoning on Paradise Island, and now freezing and starving in the middle of nowhere! Of *course* it's not romantic. What am I going to say tomorrow when we're filming? I'll have to admit that I've changed my mind and that I don't believe in romance any more.'

Simon looked at her in concern. He ought to have been pleased that she had seen sense and come round to his way of thinking, but it felt all wrong. Clara's shining belief in romance was part of her. He didn't like it when she was sensible and rational.

'You're just tired and hungry,' he said. 'You'll feel better when Ted gets here and you've had something to eat.'

But three hours crawled by and there was still

no sign of the van. Clara gnawed the inside of her cheek. 'Do you think they've been in some terrible accident?'

'No,' said Simon. 'I think they're sensibly holed up in a comfortable hotel somewhere rather than drive through the snow in the dark.'

'I wish we knew what had happened to them!'

'They'll be here in the morning. In the meantime, there's nothing we can do about it except resign ourselves to no supper.'

The torch beam was already weak, but he used it to explore upstairs, where he found ample bedding, which was something, and then he went around the living room opening and closing cupboard doors.

'What are you looking for?' asked Clara, following his progress.

'Survival rations…ah!' Simon came back to the fire with a bottle of whisky and two glasses. 'I thought a Scottish cottage had to have an emergency supply somewhere.' He held up the bottle and inspected it in the firelight. 'Half empty—I suppose you'd say half full—but it'll keep us going.'

He sloshed whisky into the glasses, and handed one to Clara. 'This will cheer you up.'

They both sat on the floor, backs against the sofa, not quite touching. Their legs were stretched out towards the fire, and the flames sent flickering shadows leaping over their faces.

Clara wasn't used to drinking whisky, she told him. She choked and spluttered at first, but she soon got the hang of it, and they drank in companionable silence for a while, their hands brushing occasionally when they set their glass on the floor between them.

Simon looked down into his glass contemplatively. He had driven for twelve hours that day and he was very hungry. Astrid would never have got him into a situation like this. On the few occasions they'd been away together, Astrid would book them into five-star hotels, and always made sure that she got a good deal by booking in advance. Simon couldn't imagine her here.

But he was oddly comfortable sitting in front of the fire in this musty old cottage. Outside, the wind worried at the windows, and the rest of the rooms were dank and bitterly cold, but within the circle of firelight it was quite cosy. They had long ago finished the mints, but the whisky was warm in his stomach and Clara was beside him, long legs sprawled in front of her, humming as she watched the fire, one of those wretched show tunes he was going to have running round his head for the rest of the week.

His eyes rested on her profile, on the tilt of her lashes, the line of her cheek, the sweet curve of her mouth, and his heart turned over. Had there really been a time when he had thought of her as ordinary? Now, every time he looked at Clara she seemed more beautiful to him. Not perfect in a cool, classic way, but with a warmth and an allure that made his senses swirl.

There was a tight feeling around his chest, and he found himself remembering what she had said in Paris. *It's about looking at the one you love and feeling your heart swelling and swelling as if it would burst.*

The way his heart felt right then.

Sensing his gaze, she glanced at him and smiled.

And that was it. The world tipped and the tight band around Simon's chest that had been keeping his emotions in check for so long snapped open, and his head reeled before the rush of feeling, as terrifying as he had feared and as exhilarating as Clara had promised.

One of these days you'll fall in love, she had said. *Then you'll know what I mean.*

Simon was glad that he was sitting down. Very carefully, he put his glass on the floor beside him. He had been afraid letting go would be like this, that the feelings would surge and slosh around out of control and that he'd be left grappling for something to hold onto. In the maelstrom, there was only one certainty.

Clara, and the fact that he loved her.

The panicky feeling subsided and the world righted itself once more, the same but with everything in a subtly different alignment. Clara was beside him and nothing else mattered. He might be tired and hungry and uncomfortable, but she was there and he was happy.

When had she become so necessary to him? Simon couldn't take his eyes off her now. Unaware of the effect of her smile, she had turned back to watch the fire, absorbed in the wavering flames.

Why her? Why Clara, with her absurdly romantic view of life, with her chaotic outfits and her infuriating singing and her exuberance? She was completely wrong for him.

And yet completely right.

He wanted to slide his hand under her hair, to see her turn towards him, her eyes widening and that smile tugging at her mouth. He wanted to draw her close, to lay her down in the firelight and make love to her until she promised that she would never leave him.

But why would she promise that? Simon picked up his glass and took a steadying sip of whisky. He had locked away his feelings after his father's death and turned inward. Clara was braver than that. She had been hurt too, but she had hidden it beneath a gaiety and a zest for life.

She had loved Matt so much. Simon's jaw tightened as he faced the truth. He could never match up to the love of Clara's life. Matt had been everything she had ever wanted. She had told him that outright. Kind, romantic, Mr Nice Guy… everything Simon wasn't, in fact.

When you love someone, you want them to be happy. That was another thing Clara had said. She wanted a man who was passionate and funny and wildly romantic, and he could never be that, Simon knew. But now the truth was out there, slapping him with his stupidity—how could he not have known how much he loved her?—he had to find a way to tell her how he felt.

He cleared his throat. 'Astrid wants us to try again.'

Clara broke off in mid hum and straightened to look at him. 'Well…that's good news,' she said a little awkwardly before she turned back to study the flames. 'I knew that was what she wanted really. What happened to Paolo?'

'She said that he was too demanding, and jealous of the time she spent at work. At first she found it flattering, she said, but after a while she wanted someone she could talk to about work. Me, in fact.'

'So what did you say?' asked Clara.

'I said no.'

'No?' The whisky slopped in her glass as she jerked in surprise. *'Why?* I thought Astrid was perfect for you?'

'I thought she was too.' Simon turned his glass between his hands, remembering the scene. 'I can't explain it. She was so practical about it. She seemed to take it for granted that we would just pick up from where we left off and go back to the way we were before, that we'd pretend that she had never said that she wanted passion and excitement and romance.'

He put the glass back on the floor beside him. 'It was only then that I realised we couldn't do that. I told her I thought we had both changed too much to pretend everything was the same.'

'Do you think you *have* changed?' Clara asked softly, and he nodded.

'The truth is that I would never have kissed you in Paris if Astrid had been really important to me. I wouldn't have wanted to kiss you on Paradise Island.' His voice deepened and his eyes rested on her face. 'I wouldn't want to kiss you now.'

Clara's eyes met his almost unwillingly, and the air between them thrummed with the memory of what that last kiss had been like.

'We did say we would try a third kiss,' she said with difficulty.

Simon's heart was pumping as he laid his hand to her cheek, twisted a strand of her silky hair around his finger. 'What if I want more than three kisses? What if I want to kiss you in London, say?'

Clara stilled. 'I don't think that would work,' she said slowly.

'Why not? Why does it matter where we are?'

'Because this isn't real,' she said, gesturing at the fire. 'The way Paradise Island wasn't real, or Paris.'

'It felt pretty real to me when I went upstairs,' said Simon. 'It's freezing up there.'

'It's real, but it's not real life,' Clara struggled to explain. 'The whole point about the places we've been is that they're special. They're places where we can step outside our normal existences for a while and do things differently, *be* different. That's what makes them so romantic.'

'Can't London be romantic?'

'For some people maybe, but not for us. London is where we both work. It's real for us. There's no way I could ever fit into your life there,' she said. 'I'd drive you crazy in five minutes.'

'You're driving me crazy now,' said Simon with a rueful smile.

'You know what I mean,' Clara said. 'We're too different. You want calmness and order, and I want music and dancing.'

Simon's heart sank. He let her hair fall and dropped his hand. She sounded so clear. *We're too different.*

What if she was right? He might have fallen in love, but he hadn't lost his mind. He still believed that shared interests were a far better basis for a successful relationship in the long run. He *did* like order. Clara probably *would* drive him crazy, just as he would drive her crazy by not singing along or sweeping her off her feet with wildly romantic gestures.

Perhaps, in the end, it was better to be sensible?

'I'm waiting for someone who isn't afraid to love me completely,' said Clara, as if she could read his mind. Pulling up her legs, she hugged her knees as she looked dreamily into the fire.

'I want someone who will take a risk for me,' she said. 'Someone who'll dance for me, sing for me... Oh, I know it's just a fantasy, I know I've probably watched too many musicals, but that's what I want. To be the star of someone's show, not an understudy or a walk-on part.'

Simon watched her profile. 'Do you really think it's possible to find someone like that?'

'Maybe not.' Her eyes were dark and huge and she turned to look at him again. 'I don't know, but I'm not prepared to settle for less than that now. I don't want to be second best again.'

Reaching out once more, Simon's hand slid beneath her hair to caress the nape of her neck and ignored the crack in his heart. 'So...it looks like we're incompatible.'

'I'm afraid so,' said Clara, but he felt her shiver

of response and she leant into his hand. 'In real life, anyway.'

'What about now? Didn't you say this isn't real life?'

A smile tugged at the corners of that lush mouth. 'No, it isn't real. For now we're both here, and we don't have to be sensible. We don't have to think about the future. We can just think about this place and this moment and the fact that there's just the two of us.'

'And that it's very cold,' Simon agreed, slowly drawing her closer. 'It's a well-established fact that the best way to keep warm is to share body heat.'

'I've heard that.' Clara smiled. 'But I know you like to test the evidence,' she said as she pulled free of his hand and clambered over him until she straddled him on the floor.

'We should do a little experiment,' she said, leaning forward to press little kisses along his jaw, and Simon's senses reeled at the feel of her, at the tickle of her hair against his cheek, the scent of her, the way she fitted so perfectly against him.

When she reached his mouth, she angled her face to kiss his lips. He tasted whisky and something that was instantly, unmistakably Clara and the tightness inside him unravelled as he sank into the heat and the piercing sweetness and the world came right at last.

'You can tell me to stop any time you're warm enough,' she murmured against his mouth and he smiled as his arms came up to pull her tight where she belonged.

'Don't stop yet,' he said. 'Don't stop at all.'

Ted, Steve and Peter arrived just before ten the next morning. 'I'm so sorry, my dears,' said Ted, hugging Clara. 'The wretched van broke down.'

'You poor things! You must have been frozen,' she said in concern. At least she and Simon had had a fire to keep them warm.

And each other.

Inside the cottage, there was no evidence of the night before. Clara had taken the bedding back upstairs, while Simon relit the fire that had died in the early hours.

Making love with him had been beyond anything Clara had ever experienced before. She told herself that it was because of the whisky and the firelight and the fact that they were marooned on a Scottish hillside, but deep down she knew that it was more than that.

She loved him. No matter how hard she tried to persuade herself that it was just a fleeting, inexplicable physical thing, the way she told Simon it was, it made no difference. Lying in his arms in the firelight, her head on his chest, Clara had listened to the slow, steady beat of his heart and her own had turned inside out. She had felt her heart expanding, while a glorious, irrevocable sense of rightness had settled in the pit of her belly.

It hadn't been like that with Matt. She had adored him, but had always sensed that she was never really the one he wanted. The more she had clutched at him, the more Matt had held back, and Clara had been permanently tense. She'd been afraid to be herself in case he realised that he didn't really love her, but in the end he had realised that anyway.

Clara knew Simon couldn't love her. She hadn't wanted him to love her, and she hadn't tried to be anything other than what she was. Perhaps that was why it felt so utterly right being with him, why she felt more herself than she had ever been before. When they had made love, the differences between them hadn't mattered. They were just two people who fitted together perfectly.

Now I understand, Clara had thought in the middle of the night. All those love songs she sang with such gusto weren't just lovely tunes. They were true.

But loving Simon didn't change anything. They wanted different things. *Needed* different things. She would irritate Simon, and he would disappoint her. His father's irresponsibility had scarred him, Clara understood that. It wasn't that he was too stubborn to let go. He *couldn't*. Letting go was too much of a risk for him, and she couldn't spend her life being careful.

So Clara told herself that this short time with him would be enough. That morning when they woke up tangled in the covers in front of the ashes in the fireplace, they had made love once more, but when they got up, they both knew that it was over.

The power had come on in the middle of the night, startling them both with the glare of light bulbs. Clara had a hot shower, and mentally braced herself to hide the love that wanted to spill out of her. But it wouldn't be fair to tell Simon. It would just make everything awkward. Already, she could see that he had withdrawn behind his defences. That was fine, Clara told herself. It would be easier to say goodbye that way.

Now Ted and the crew were here, and she had a job to do.

'Did you get any sleep?' she asked Ted as Steve and Peter started unloading the van.

'Oh, yes,' said Ted. 'The mechanic fixed it, but by then it was so late, and it was snowing, so we stopped at the next pub and set off first thing this morning. It was surprisingly comfortable.'

'I told you so,' Simon said to Clara, who put her hands on her hips and glared at Ted.

'I was imagining you'd skidded off the road and were freezing to death on some isolated hillside, and all the while you were tucked up in a warm pub!'

'I did try to ring you, but I couldn't get through.' Ted tucked his arm through hers. 'How did you two get on?'

'We were starving,' said Clara lightly, 'but otherwise we survived, didn't we, Simon?'

She thought they both looked perfectly normal, but Ted's eyes sharpened as he looked from one to the other. 'So, are you ready to shoot?' was all he said though.

'Not until we've had breakfast.'

It was a strange day. The snow had cleared overnight, leaving a dusting of white on the heather. Having arrived in the dark, Clara was unprepared for the sight of the massive hills looming around the cottage, and she had actually gasped when she'd stepped out of the cottage that morning. The photos on the Internet hadn't done the scenery justice, and it made a spectacular backdrop for the outside shots Ted wanted.

Clara and Simon sat on a great granite boulder with the hills behind them, while Peter struggled to keep the boom in place above their heads in the bitter wind. They stuck to the arguments that they had played out in Paris and on Paradise Island, but all the time Clara was remembering the feel of Simon's body, the wicked pleasure of his hands, the darkness and the heat that had burned between them.

She knew Simon was remembering too. Sometimes she would catch his eye and a crackle of awareness passed between them. The stern line of his mouth would soften then, and he would cough and raise his hand to hide the hint of a smile, until Ted yelled at him that he was spoiling the shot and they would have to do that bit again.

'Sorry, Ted.'

It was so cold that they were all glad when Ted decreed some fireside shots, but it was even harder then to maintain a professional distance. They were sitting in exactly the same spot where they had made love the night before, and it was impossible not to remember how it had been, impossible not to wish that it could be just the two of them again.

Clara was afraid that Ted would make some comment about them not concentrating—he could be very cutting when he wanted—but when he said nothing, she presumed that she and Simon had brushed through it without giving themselves away.

At last it was over. 'And…it's a wrap!' Ted spread his arms in his best Hollywood movie mogul mode. 'Well done, my dears. Let's all have an enormous drink!'

Now that filming was over, they could relax. The power stayed on, so they cooked all the food and drank all the wine Clara had packed for two nights.

Clara refused to think about the fact that there would be no reason to see Simon again. Roland had been lukewarm, to say the least, about the idea of follow-up documentaries on Simon's micro-finance projects. 'Not exactly a sexy subject, is it?' he had said.

When Clara had steeled herself to tell Simon, he had been phlegmatic. 'It was worth a try,' he said.

If only Roland had leapt on the idea! He could make things happen when he wanted them to, and they could have had a commission lined up already. Then this wouldn't have been the end. She could have driven back to London with Simon and, instead of saying goodbye, she would have had the perfect excuse to call him. *I'll be in touch*, she could have said, and then they would have been working together again and then—

And then what? Clara interrupted herself. Nothing would really have changed. Everything she had said the night before was true. She and Simon were too different to make it work. Astrid might not be the right one for him, but there would be someone else, someone more sensible and suitable than Clara.

Better to accept it now. Simon would drive her back to London the next day and that would be it. Oh, perhaps they would have a polite chat over a screening of the preview, or a stilted phone call to inform him of the release date, but there would be no more trips, no more times alone.

No more making love.

But she had known all along that it would end, Clara reminded herself. There was only ever the moment, and she would live for it now. So she tucked her feelings away, the way she had always done, and smiled brightly and probably drank more than she should.

OK, she *definitely* drank more than she should. All she really remembered the next day was standing on the table and using a wooden spoon as a microphone as she belted out show tunes, cheered on by Steve and Peter. Simon hadn't encouraged her, but she knew that his eyes were on her and, although he shook his head in mock despair, he was smiling.

CHAPTER TEN

SIMON was unsympathetic about her hangover the next morning. 'It serves you right,' he said. 'Does this mean no singing down the motorway?'

Clara held her aching head. 'No anything,' she croaked.

It was a very quiet journey. They listened to Radio 4 the whole way, just as Simon had wanted to do when they drove up. Except he couldn't appreciate it as much as he should have done.

This time there was no incessant singing and humming, no tapping of the feet or dancing of the hands. No chomping of crisps. No low, wicked laugh, no teasing smile. It wasn't the same when she was quiet. He even began to wish that she would sing again, and who would ever have thought that?

Simon glanced across to where she was huddled in the seat, her face wan and her eyes closed, and he had to suppress a grin at the thought of her the night before, up on that table, singing into the wooden spoon and kicking her legs.

God, he was going to miss her.

Simon held grimly onto the wheel and tried not to think about how empty his life was going to be from now on. He couldn't regret their night together but how long was it going to be before he stopped aching for what he was missing? How long before he forgot the heat and the wildness of losing control? The moment he had that sweet, luscious body under his hands, he had been lost, all sensible thought obliterated as his mind went blank and black with desire, and his heart shifted at the memory.

One night, that was what they had agreed. It was sensible. It was practical. It was better for both of them.

Clara was a very special person, and she deserved to be happy, thought Simon. She had made it clear that one night was all that she had wanted. He couldn't give her the fantasy she craved, and she didn't want to settle for less.

So she would go her way, and he would get back to his nice, ordered life and that would be that. There was no point in telling her how he felt. It would just make things more difficult.

Simon told himself that it was all for the best. He liked it quiet, didn't he? There would be no more singing, none of those smiles that made his heart lurch alarmingly. No illogical arguments, no rolling of the eyes, no fear that any moment she would break into a dance routine.

No Clara.

There was a space right outside her flat. Simon parked and switched off the engine. On that busy London street, the silence was suffocating.

'Well,' said Clara.

'Well,' said Simon.

The air was clogged with tension. He undid his seat belt for want of anything else to do. 'I suppose this is it,' he said after a moment.

'Yes.' Her voice was strained. 'At least, there's no more filming. Ted will edit it now, and we'll record the voice-over. Obviously we'll let you know when it's done, and let you have a preview copy.'

'Fine.'

'But you've done your bit.' Clara cleared her throat. 'I know you didn't want to do it, but I'm really grateful to you, Simon. We would never have been able to make the programme without you.'

Simon shifted round in his seat so that he could look at her. 'It wasn't so bad,' he said slowly.

The truth was that it had been the most fun he could remember having since before his father died.

And look how that had turned out.

The heat and sweetness and the need that had engulfed him at the cottage had blotted out all else, but now the reminder of where too much fun could lead jerked Simon back to reality just as he was on the point of begging to see her again.

Better to call an end to this—whatever *this* was—now. It would just get complicated and end in Clara being disappointed, and he couldn't bear to do that to her.

Clara would always have a good time. She had a zest for life that Simon both yearned for and feared. She needed someone who could enjoy the good times with her and not spoil things by pointing out the practicalities or considering the consequences.

Someone who wasn't him.

'I enjoyed it,' he said.

'I'm glad.' Clara's smile was uneven as she un-clipped her seat belt and reached for the door. 'I'd better go.'

He didn't want to let her go. 'Clara…'

She turned back, still holding the door handle.

'I did enjoy it,' he said as if she had said she didn't believe him. 'And that night—'

'You don't need to say anything,' she interrupted him. 'That night was fantastic, but we both know it wouldn't be like that again.'

'Wouldn't it?'

'I mean, look at us,' she said, gesturing from Simon's neat navy Guernsey to her layers of mismatched colours and patterns, topped off with the vividly striped scarf she always wore. 'We couldn't be more different.'

'It didn't matter at the cottage.'

Clara bit her lip. 'And it might not matter tomorrow, or next week, or the week after that, but sooner or later, it would. You taught me that,' she said. 'You have to find someone who shares your goals and your interests and fits into your life. We've had some romantic moments, but moments are all they are.'

She was right. It was what he had said all along, Simon knew, but it sounded all wrong coming out of her mouth.

'Well, I enjoyed them,' he said.

Clara's brave smile evaporated from her face. 'Me too,' she whispered.

'Goodbye, Clara.' Simon leant across and gently

kissed her mouth, and she laid her palm against his cheek and kissed him back. It was short and achingly sweet. A farewell kiss.

'Goodbye, Simon.' Her eyes were shimmering with tears as she dropped her hand, and his heart shook with wanting her.

Before he could jerk her back into his arms, she was out of the car, grabbing her bag from the back seat, running up the steps to the front door. He watched her put the key in the door, push it open. At the last minute she turned and lifted a hand to him. Simon lifted a hand in return.

Then she went inside and closed the door.

She was gone.

'You can't show this!' Clara looked from Ted to Roland in horror. They had just shown her the preview copy of *Romance: Fact or Fiction?*, now titled *How to Fall in Love (When You Really Don't Want To)*.

'Lovey, it's a great programme,' said Ted gently.

'It's not! It's nothing like we planned. This is a completely different film! It's…*private.*'

Clara was near to tears. She hadn't been looking forward to watching the preview, knowing it would bring back bittersweet memories of

Simon, but she had never dreamed that it would be this bad.

She knew that she had made the right decision. Going their separate ways was the sensible thing to do. Sometimes she saw Simon on the news, and he looked cool and contained and like the grown-up that he was, while she was still muddling along, not knowing anything except the fact that she missed him.

Nothing was right without him. She couldn't dance any more because there was a leaden weight inside her that threw her off balance, and her heart was too bleak for her to be able to sing. Always before she had been able to bury her feelings beneath a light-hearted veneer, but not this time.

This time it was too hard.

Getting through every day was a chore. Clara had thrown herself into work, and put in long hours while Ted and Roland were closeted in the editing suite. Her job had been her only consolation.

Until now.

Clara turned an accusing glare on Ted. 'Why didn't you warn me?'

'I didn't think you'd like it.' Ted had the grace

to blush. 'I thought that if you saw the finished result, you might realise what a great story it is now.'

Oh, she could see that. It was a clever piece of film-making. All the locations were lovingly shot. Ted had taken everything she and Simon had said for the camera and edited it so that the arguments came across as an interesting, engaging debate. He had made the programme that they had planned.

But he hadn't stopped there. Their set pieces were intercut with shots of Simon and Clara when they thought they were off camera.

There they were in Paris. Simon putting his jacket around her shoulders on the Pont Neuf, rolling his eyes as she sang herself into a confident mood. Absorbed in each other in the Montmartre bistro. Dancing close together in the club. Ted took his camera wherever he went. Why hadn't she remembered that?

There they were sitting on that granite boulder, the wind whipping Clara's hair around her face. She held it back with one hand and looked at Simon with her heart in her eyes. And Simon, watching her as she danced on the table. How could she possibly have thought their body language wasn't revealing? They might as well have hung out a sign that they had slept together.

There they were on Paradise Island, on the end of the dock. Clara supposed she should be grateful Ted hadn't filmed her throwing up, but he had been there later because there they were on the beach, watching the sunset together.

Kissing.

It was dark, and not that clear, but there was no doubt about what they were doing.

Clara's face was hot. 'What were you doing spying on us on the beach?' she said furiously to Ted. 'That was just pervy!'

'I just happened to be getting some establishing shots of the sunset,' he said, but his eyes slid away from hers.

'Hah!'

'Clara, I know how it seems, but it was just so clear what the real story was,' Ted tried to explain. 'Simon was saying one thing and it was obvious that he really believed it, but at the same time he was feeling something else entirely. I could tell right from the start that he was falling in love with you.'

Ted didn't bother to say that it had been just

as obvious that she had been falling in love with Simon at the same time.

'It wasn't like that,' said Clara dully.

'You only need to watch the programme to see that he is.'

'You don't understand!' Clara took a breath and fought to stay calm. 'Yes, we had a fling, but that's all it was. That's not how Simon is. You know what his reputation is. If you show this, he'll be a laughing stock! It's wrong!'

She turned imploringly to Roland, who was leaning back in his chair, picking his nails. 'You can't do this!'

'I think you'll find I can,' he said. 'This is all very sweet, but Simon Valentine signed a release and there's nothing in there about having to approve what goes out.'

'He didn't know you were going to put this... this *travesty* together!'

'Tough,' said Roland. 'They're going to lap this up at Channel 16. I've got to admit that I had my doubts when Ted suggested you as a stand-in for Stella in Paris,' he admitted frankly, 'but it's turned out brilliantly. I said to him when he first showed me the edits, "I think you've got something here, mate." Didn't I, Ted?'

Ted nodded. The traitor. He looked uncomfortable. As well he might, thought Clara, clenching her fists in frustration. She knew Ted would hate upsetting her, but he was a passionate film maker and if he believed in this programme, she wouldn't shift him.

'Look, this is going to turn out fine,' Roland said. 'I think we'll get more commissions on the back of this one, and you can produce them if you want. Get your own production assistant. How about that?'

Clara stared at him. She felt sick. Her dream job, in return for letting them expose Simon to the media wolves. Simon, who was so famously controlled, so self-contained, his guard down for everyone to jeer over. The press would have a field day. It had been bad enough for him when Stella had spread those silly rumours, but this would be on television for everyone to see and laugh about.

'No,' she said.

'No what?'

'No, I won't let you do it,' she said clearly. 'Simon may have signed a release, but I didn't. I won't give you permission to show this.'

Roland's face darkened. He turned to Ted. 'She didn't sign a release?'

'It's Clara's job to make sure they get signed,' said Ted nervously.

'Oh, that's just great!' snarled Roland. 'Then it's a straight choice, Clara. Sign the release and keep your job, or take a walk.'

'Roland—' Ted started to protest, but Clara didn't wait to hear or stop to think. Pushing back her chair, she snatched up her bag and jacket.

'I'll take the walk.'

Clara sat at the table in her parents' comfortably shabby Oxford kitchen. Outside, it was a soft spring day, but the blue sky and the tubs of cheerful daffodils weren't enough to stop the world looking grey. Dispiritedly, she scrolled through the 'jobs vacant' on her laptop. She had to find a job somehow.

Television was out. Roland had plenty of contacts in the media, and she knew he had put the word out that she was unreliable. Competition was cut-throat as it was. She'd be lucky if she ever got another job in production, Clara thought miserably.

If she didn't get a job soon, she would have to

tell Allegra couldn't afford to pay rent any more. Staying in London had been too painful, and she had come home to Oxford for a few days to regroup. Her parents had welcomed her back with their usual vaguely baffled kindness.

'Of course you can stay,' her mother had said, deep in an article about ecclesiastical reform in the sixteenth century. 'What about your job, though?'

'I told you,' said Clara. 'I had to leave.'

'Oh, dear. I thought you liked working in television too.'

Clara supposed it was something that her mother remembered what it was she'd been doing.

'I did,' she said.

She missed her job. She missed working with Ted. She missed Allegra and the flat and the in-depth discussions about Saturday night TV.

But, most of all, she missed Simon. Ted's film had been a shock. She hadn't realised their feelings were quite so obvious. A little bit of Clara had rejoiced to see Simon falling for her, of course—the bit that had urged her to pick up the phone, to call him and tell him how she felt. But a saner, more sensible part held her back.

Simon might be attracted to her, but he hadn't

changed. Neither of them had changed. He was still logical, practical, a man who needed order and control, and she was still a girl who needed to be loved completely. Simon would never be able to do that. Clara understood just how carefully he guarded his emotions. She needed more than he was able to give, and it was better to accept that now than hope and hope the way she had done with Matt.

Anyway, it wasn't really love, whatever Ted's film made it look like. It was an attraction, Clara decided. A physical thing. That wasn't the same. But there was still a tight band around chest, making it hard to breathe properly. Her back was still stiff, her limbs still rigid, her heart locked down.

Ted had been in touch, miserably torn and desperate to make amends. He was worried about her. When Matt had left her for Sophie, it was Ted who had dragged her along to a *Sound of Music* singalong, and her spirits had been instantly boosted, but this time Clara didn't even have the heart for that.

Her father had disappeared to answer the doorbell. He was expecting a PhD student, and had forgotten that he still had a piece of toast in his hand. Her mother was sitting at the other end of the table, drinking coffee and marking essays.

'What are you doing today, Clara?' she asked absently.

'Looking for a job,' said Clara. London had too many painful memories. Perhaps she should try and find something in Oxford? It would be humiliating to have to move back in with her parents, but what did a bit of humiliation matter now?

'Why don't you think about doing a degree?'

'What in? The collected works of Rodgers and Hammerstein?'

'There must be something you want to do.'

See Simon. Touch Simon. Be with Simon. Did they offer a degree in that?

'I don't think I'm university material, Mum.' Clara sighed and slumped back in her chair. 'I don't seem to be very good at anything.'

Her mother lifted her head at that and inspected her daughter over the top of her glasses. 'Oh, I don't think that's the case at all,' she said but before Clara could ask her what she meant, her father wandered back in, eating his toast.

'What have you done with your student?'

'It wasn't her. It's some man for you, Clara,' he said vaguely.

'Me? But nobody knows I'm here.' Ted might have guessed, but her parents knew him well and not even her father was vague enough to not recognize him. 'Are you sure it was me he wanted?'

'I may be a little absent-minded sometimes, but I'm not senile,' her father said, pouring himself some more coffee. 'Of course it was you.'

Puzzled, Clara pushed back her chair and went to the door.

And there was Simon.

Her heart leapt with joy and the world, which had been dully monochrome and all askew, abruptly righted itself and sprang back into colour.

'Simon!'

She drank in the sight of him on the doorstep. He was looking positively casual in an open-necked shirt and jacket, but otherwise he was wonderfully *Simon*. She loved the austere angles of his face, the stern mouth that made her knees go weak, the quiet solidity of him.

She wanted to throw herself into his arms, but the strained look in his eyes, the tautness around his mouth, made her pause.

'Is everything OK?'

'Fine.' Simon cleared his throat. 'That is…fine.

I just came by because…well, I wondered if you had a summer house here,' he finished in a rush.

Clara's jaw dropped. She didn't know what she had been expecting, but it wasn't that. 'A *summer house*?'

'Do you?'

Was this a peculiarly vivid dream? 'There's a shed in the back garden,' she said cautiously.

'The back garden. That'll do fine.'

'Whatever for?'

'Could we go there now?' he asked tensely. 'If you're not too busy?'

Clara stared at him. 'Simon, are you sure you're all right? You're behaving very strangely.'

'I know,' he said. 'It's just there's something I need to do before I lose my nerve.'

'In the shed?' But she stood back and Simon stepped past her into the house.

Still half convinced that this was a dream, Clara led him down the narrow Victorian tiled hall to the back door. They passed the open door of the kitchen, where her parents were having an erudite discussion about Derrida interspersed with requests to pass the marmalade.

There was a flash of the old Simon as he raised his brows at Clara. 'They mixed up the babies at the hospital,' she whispered. 'My real parents are out there somewhere slumped in front of the television and watching soaps.'

Neither of her parents was much of a gardener, and the long walled garden was rather neglected. The borders were straggly and overgrown, and dandelions were starting to sprout in the grass and between the worn stones of the patio.

'That's the shed,' said Clara, pointing. It was faded and listing slightly to one side, and she couldn't imagine what Simon wanted with it.

'It's all right. This will do.' Simon was looking around the patio, moving a pot out of the way and pulling out a rickety garden chair. 'Sit down,' he said as he steered Clara towards it.

'Simon, what's going on?'

'Just a minute.' He took a deep breath, and opened his mouth. And then closed it again.

'What?' Clara was getting really worried.

Simon cleared his throat savagely. 'Sorry,' he said. 'I'll start again.'

Another breath and then, to Clara's astonishment, he launched into a cracked and uncertain rendition from *The Sound of Music*.

A dazzling hope blurred Clara's eyes with tears. It was unmistakably *Climb Every Mountain*, even if he forgot the words halfway through and had to improvise.

And he was dancing! True, Simon was no Nureyev, but he was definitely shuffling from side to side and every now and then he even tried a twirl. His expression was intent, and he was frowning as he tried to remember the words and coordinate with the movements. Several times he found himself facing the wrong way, and had to turn round hastily and pick up his routine again.

Clara covered her mouth with her hand. She didn't know whether to laugh or cry. Simon was there, it was really him, and he was dancing for her.

And then he was holding out his hand, inviting her to dance with him, drawing her up from her chair. Smiling through her tears, she let him swing her round until he came to a halt with a flourish.

'...your dree-eam,' he finished tunelessly and looked into Clara's eyes at last with a mixture of relief, trepidation and excruciating embarrassment.

'Simon,' she said, starry-eyed. 'You were singing. You were *dancing*.'

'I'm not very good, I know.'

'That was the best version of *Climb Every Mountain* I've ever heard.' Her voice cracked a little as she put her arms around his neck. 'The *best*,' she whispered in his ear as he pulled her close but, before he could kiss her there was a burst of applause from the kitchen window.

Clara's parents, evidently distracted from Derrida by Simon's singing, were beaming broadly and clapping.

'Excellent! Very well done!'

'Clara's always needed someone who will dance with her,' said her father when Clara introduced Simon to them.

'I'm not really much of a dancer,' he confessed.

'You looked like you were doing fine to us.' Which just went to show how much her parents knew about dancing.

Her mother, it appeared, had noticed more than Clara had thought. 'Are you the reason Clara has been so unhappy lately?' she demanded, regarding Simon with the severity she reserved for students who hadn't prepared for a seminar.

'We don't like Clara being unhappy,' her father added. 'She was born for laughter. The rest of us have our research, but Clara has an ability to enjoy life that we've always envied.'

Clara was astounded. All those years when she had felt inadequate and excluded in the family, and all the time *they* had been envying *her*? Could it be true? 'But I thought...' She broke off as the doorbell rang.

Her mother clicked her tongue. 'That'll be your student, Michael. You'd better go and let her in.' She turned back to Clara and Simon with a twinkle. 'If there are to be any more song and dance routines, you'll have to keep the noise down, I'm afraid.'

'I think once was enough,' said Simon ruefully.

He took Clara's hands as her parents disappeared. '*Was* once enough, Clara?'

'Yes,' she said, her fingers tightening around his. She knew just how much that dance must have cost him. 'Oh, Simon, I can't believe you did that for me!'

'It was the only way I could think of to tell you how much I love you,' he said. 'I remembered what you said at that cottage about wanting to be the star of someone's show, and I wanted to tell you that you'll always be the star of mine.'

Clara's throat was so tight, she could hardly talk. 'Simon...' was all she managed to choke out.

'I love you, Clara,' he said, his eyes locked on

hers. 'If you want me to sing and dance for you every day, I will.'

'You don't need to do that,' said Clara, finding her voice at last. Drawing her hands free, she put them on his shoulders, feeling his strength and his solidity. Letting herself believe that that was really happening.

'You don't need to dance for me, or sing for me, Simon. You just need to be you. You just need to be there. You just need to love me.'

'I can do that,' said Simon, so obviously relieved that she laughed, giddy with happiness, and he laughed too and kissed her. Wild joy surged along her veins, and she wrapped her arms around his neck and kissed him back.

'I missed you,' she mumbled at last between kisses.

'I missed you too.'

He held her tightly, and she leant against him with a great sigh of contentment. 'I imagined you getting on with your quiet, comfortable life,' she confessed.

'I tried to,' said Simon, 'but it wasn't comfortable without you. It was too quiet. There was no one to distract me or to sing or to make me laugh.'

'Why didn't you say anything?'

'Because I was imagining *you* having a great time without me. I thought you'd be out dancing or singing on tables, and I couldn't imagine why you would possibly want to spend time with someone conventional like me.'

Clara's body shook with laughter. 'You're never that, Simon. No one truly conventional would have come and demanded to dance in my parents' garden shed!' She pulled slightly away from him. 'What was the shed about anyway?'

'I wanted a summer house, like in *The Sound of Music*.'

She looked at him in amazement. 'How on earth did you know about that? I didn't think you'd even seen the film?'

'I have now. I missed all those stupid songs you sing so much that I was actually reduced to buying the DVD!'

'No?' Clara was delighted. 'So that's where you learnt the words! And how did you work out the dance routine?'

'That was my mother,' Simon admitted, pulling her back against him. 'I was desperate and I couldn't think of anyone else to ask. I don't know anyone else who dances. She enjoyed herself enormously, and said that if you were prepared to talk to me after seeing the way I danced, you must love me.'

'She's right,' said Clara, kissing him. 'I do.'

'Now you know why I was so nervous when I arrived. I was terrified I would lose my nerve.'

'I'm glad you didn't. I'll never forget that dance on the patio!' Her smile faded. 'Seriously, I know how hard that was for you, Simon.'

'I've learnt that letting go doesn't have to mean losing everything,' said Simon. 'You've taught me that. Sometimes, taking a risk and letting go means you can win everything you've ever wanted.' His pale eyes were warmer than Clara had ever seen them. How could she ever have thought of them as cold? 'Sometimes you have to leave your safe home and climb that mountain, in fact.'

Clara laughed and pressed closer, breathing in the wonderful, familiar scent of him. 'Who would have thought you'd ever be quoting from *The Sound of Music*?'

'I'm not the only one who's taken a risk, Clara.' Simon's expression grew serious. 'Ted came to see me. He told me that you'd refused the producer job Roland offered you and walked out of MediaOchre.'

Her eyes slid from his. 'Yes, well, we had a… difference of opinion.'

'Clara, you really wanted to be a producer.'

'Oh, well, you know I'm not very good at sticking with things.'

Simon drew her down onto the patio wall and turned her face to his. 'You gave up that job for me,' he said. 'Ted showed me the film.'

She flushed at the memory. 'It was *awful*, wasn't it? But don't worry, they won't be able to show it. I refused to sign a release so, unless they make the film the way they originally planned it, they're stuck.'

'I know. Ted told me.' Simon smiled crookedly. 'I said I was happy for the film to go out as it was if you agreed. I promised him I'd try and persuade you to change your mind.'

'What?' Clara jerked upright to stare at him.

'Ted's right. It's a great film.'

'But it's so…*intimate.*'

'It's *true*, Clara. There I am, fighting it all the way, and it's clear as houses that I'm falling in love with you. I'm standing there saying one thing, and the viewer can see that I'm doing the opposite.'

'I can't understand why you're being so reasonable about this,' said Clara. 'It's embarrassing.'

'I'm not embarrassed to love you,' said Simon. 'Yes, I look a fool, but that's true too! And let's face it, you won the argument. Romance won out over logic, fair and square.'

'I don't think I did win,' she said thoughtfully, settling back into the curve of his arm. 'I didn't fall in love with you because we were in Paris, or on that beautiful beach. I fell in love because even when things went wrong, you were there for me, to hold the umbrella, or fetch a bucket, to give me your jacket or stop me worrying.'

She tilted her face up to his. 'And what did I ever do for you except drag you out into the rain and strand you halfway up a mountain with no food and throw up all over you?'

'They're all precious memories to me,' he said, straight-faced.

'Those places weren't romantic in the end,' said Clara. 'But a truly terrible dance routine…*that* was romantic. I don't need a dance partner, Simon. I need someone who's prepared to take a risk for me, someone who'll grit his teeth and make a fool of himself to show me that he loves me.'

'And I need someone who'll make me laugh and push me out of my comfort zone and make me *feel*,' said Simon, gathering her into him for a long, sweet kiss.

'I think we should let them show that programme, Clara,' he said much later when he lifted his head. 'Tell Roland he can do it if he makes you a producer.'

'It would be good,' said Clara, tempted. 'I've missed my job.'

'I didn't think much of the ending, though, did you? Why don't we suggest a better one?'

'Hmm, there's a thought. We could sing in a music festival and then escape over some mountains. That would give it the drama it's rather lacking at the moment.'

'It's an interesting idea,' Simon agreed, 'but I was thinking that it might be a nice touch to end with something a bit more tame. Like a wedding, for instance.'

Clara primmed her lips, pretending to consider the idea, but her eyes danced. 'A wedding?'

'Yes. I thought it would tie up a few loose ends. Of course, it would mean us getting married,' he said. 'Do you think that would work?'

'Do you know, I think it might,' she said, kissing him. 'I think it would make a perfect ending.'

'Or a perfect beginning,' said Simon, kissing her back.

In the garden, a blackbird started to sing, a pure trill of joy. Clara felt the sunshine on her shoulders and Simon's warm arm around her, and when she pressed her face into his throat and breathed in the scent of his skin, she thought she would shatter with happiness.

Now she knew what Julie Andrews had been singing about when she wondered what she had done to deserve being loved by the Captain.

Clara thought about Simon, about the serious, formidably intelligent, heart-shakingly attractive man he was, and it seemed so incredible that he could actually love her that she wondered if she really were dreaming. They were so different. It was hardly any time since he had categorically refused to have anything to do with her. No, no, no, no, no, *no*, he had said.

'Simon, are you *sure* you want to marry me?' she asked, and she felt him smile against her temple.

'Yes,' said Simon.

Tonight on Channel 16
8.00 p.m. How to Fall in Love (When You Really Don't Want To) *****
   Surprisingly absorbing examination of

romance and whether it really exists, with Simon Valentine, whose incisive analysis of the financial situation has won him a legion of female fans—all of whom are likely to be disappointed by the chemistry that fairly sizzles between him and his co-presenter. Worth watching just for the ending. Have a hankie handy!

* * * * *

Mills & Boon® Large Print
May 2012

THE MAN WHO RISKED IT ALL
Michelle Reid

THE SHEIKH'S UNDOING
Sharon Kendrick

THE END OF HER INNOCENCE
Sara Craven

THE TALK OF HOLLYWOOD
Carole Mortimer

MASTER OF THE OUTBACK
Margaret Way

THEIR MIRACLE TWINS
Nikki Logan

RUNAWAY BRIDE
Barbara Hannay

WE'LL ALWAYS HAVE PARIS
Jessica Hart

Mills & Boon® Large Print
June 2012

AN OFFER SHE CAN'T REFUSE
Emma Darcy

AN INDECENT PROPOSITION
Carol Marinelli

A NIGHT OF LIVING DANGEROUSLY
Jennie Lucas

A DEVILISHLY DARK DEAL
Maggie Cox

THE COP, THE PUPPY AND ME
Cara Colter

BACK IN THE SOLDIER'S ARMS
Soraya Lane

MISS PRIM AND THE BILLIONAIRE
Lucy Gordon

DANCING WITH DANGER
Fiona Harper

mL

5- 12